"Hey, look out!" someone yelled.

Huh? Nikki glanced up and spotted some unsuspecting boy about her age wearing an orange T-shirt and a baseball cap in her direct path. She swerved quickly to the left, just missing him. "Sorry!" she called back to him.

The boy removed his hat, exposing an extreme buzz cut. Even from this distance Nikki could see his striking blue eyes. They were big and round and surprised-looking. *Oh my God, he's so hot,* she thought, *and I almost killed him!*

i ♥ bikinis

He's With Me by Tamara Summers

Island Summer by Jeanine Le Ny

What's Hot by Caitlyn Davis

i ♥ bikinis

Island Summer

Jeanine Le Ny

Point

For my big Italian (and French) family —JLN

No part of this work may be reproduced, stored in a retrieval system, or transmitted in any form or by any means, electronic, mechanical, photocopying, recording, or otherwise, without written permission of the publisher. For information regarding permission, write to Scholastic Inc., Attention: Permissions Department, 557 Broadway, New York, NY 10012.

ISBN-13: 978-0-439-91851-0
ISBN-10: 0-439-91851-0

Copyright © 2007 by Jeanine Le Ny

SCHOLASTIC, POINT, and associated logos are trademarks and/or registered trademarks of Scholastic Inc.

12 11 10 9 8 7 6 5 4 3 2   7 8 9 10 11 12/0
01
Printed in the U.S.A.
First printing, June 2007

Island Summer

chapter 1

"Blair, I can't go with you to Bella Island. It's my dog, Rocky. He ... he's come down with, um, *scurvy*." Nicole Devita stared intently at her reflection in the mirror, hoping to make the excuse seem *somewhat* believable. No such luck.

She glanced back at the healthy brown mutt sprawled on her bedroom rug happily chomping on a squeaky plastic shoe. So what else was Nikki supposed to say? That her parents had suddenly — at the last minute — decided that, at age fifteen, she wasn't *mature* enough to go on a fabulous vacation without them? Which, in all honesty, was the main point. To go *without* them.

Nikki whirled around to lean on the white dresser attached to her mirror and let her gaze fall across the overstuffed navy duffel on her lemon-colored bedspread. It was all zipped and sausagelike, ready to be lugged to the resort island where pretty much everyone from Richfield Academy for Girls would be lounging for the summer. That included her good friend Blair Winchester, who had invited Nikki to stay at the family "cottage" complete with maid, cook, and personal Pilates instructor.

"I can't *believe* they waited until this morning to tell me," Nikki muttered, getting angry all over again.

It was bad enough that Nikki and Blair — and the rest of the girls at the Academy, for that matter — came from alternate universes. Nikki didn't live in one of the grand historic homes of Richfield or on a sprawling estate just outside the village like her classmates did. Instead, Nikki resided on Pelican Island, which was famous for, well, *pelicans*, and for commercial fishing, not to mention the faint stench of gutted sardines.

The thing was, Nicole could survive without having the whole Paris Hilton lifestyle going on like her friends, but why *couldn't* she spend a couple of weeks away from her family? It's not as if Nicole, aka Miss A-student-who's-never-seen-a-day-of-detention-*ever*, had given her parents a reason to distrust her. No, as far as she was concerned, an excuse about a dog with scurvy was far less humiliating than admitting to her parents' overprotective insanity.

"Colie! You'd better get going if you want to catch your friend at the dock!" her seventeen-year-old brother, Paul, yelled from somewhere downstairs.

"It's *Nikki*!" Nicole shouted back. And it had been for two years, though Paul — along with the rest of her family — hadn't seemed to notice.

Nicole gave Rocky a quick pat on the head before thudding down to the family's small, sunny kitchen. She found Paul standing in front of the fridge in his pajama bottoms, taking a swig from the orange juice container. His fraternal twin, Vince, was perched on the green Formica counter and making that annoying *ummmm, ummmm* noise as he wolfed down a huge bowl of cornflakes.

Vince, a man of few words, glanced up at Nicole, grimaced, and let out a belch in her direction.

"Nice," Nikki commented, swiping the OJ from Paul, who smiled, then ripped one in her face. *"Mmmuuuurrrrp!"*

Ew. Sour juice and onions. Nikki wrinkled her

3

nose. "Can't you guys wait until I'm gone before you release your noxious fumes?" she asked, reaching around Vince to grab a glass from the cabinet.

"Consider yourself lucky I passed on the second helping of cauliflower last night," Vince responded. He shoved in a spoonful of cereal and began to chew. "Ummm, ummm . . ."

"*I* didn't." Paul clenched his stomach dramatically. "Uh-oh. You'd better get out of here, Colie." He doubled over. "Oh, ohhhhhh . . ."

"You're disgusting!" Nicole cried and darted outside through the side door. Hysterical laughter erupted from inside the kitchen, along with several fake farting noises.

Nicole rolled her eyes, knowing full well that this was it: This was her summer right here in all its glory. She turned to leave the house.

"Colie, hold up." Paul pushed open the old screen door and stretched in the doorway. "I almost forgot. Mom and Dad want you to go by the store after you say good-bye to your friend."

"Yeah, okay," Nikki said. They probably wanted to ground her for her "attitude" this morning. But who could blame her for being in a bad mood? "See you later," she told Paul, who released the screen door with a slam.

Nikki trekked through the grass past the colorful lilies Dad had planted on the side of their house, then down a short path to the sidewalk. It wasn't long before she was crossing the small concrete bridge that led to the mainland. She passed underneath the two enormous gray open-winged, openmouthed pelican statues that could be considered either welcoming or disturbing, depending on how you saw the world. An arched sign poised between the pelicans read WELCOME TO PELICAN ISLAND, which always struck Nikki as funny since nobody from the mainland ever traveled over that bridge and the people from Pelican seemed to like it that way.

Once on the other side, Nikki took a sharp right, passing the round blue-and-white Bella Island jitney ticket booth, and headed down the long crowded pier toward the ferry. She spotted Blair in the distance, leaning casually on a rail in cute white shorts and a matching tank with her superlong blond hair pulled into a sleek ponytail.

"Hi, Blair," Nikki said, approaching.

"Hey, girl. My bags are already on the boat."

Blair slid her enormous black sunglasses to the top of her head and spied Nikki's empty hands. "Where's your stuff?" She searched behind Nikki, probably looking for a porter or something.

"I have some bad news, B." Nikki took a deep breath and spilled it. "Vito and Stella changed their minds. I can't go."

"What?" Blair gasped. "But we have the whole summer planned. Pilates every morning, tennis on Tuesdays and Thursdays, poolhopping and the beach club every other day . . . and how am I supposed to flirt with the hotties from Berkley Prep if I don't have my best friend to back me up?" she asked, swinging her shiny ponytail over her shoulder for emphasis.

Nikki loved the fact that Blair had no clue about how gorgeous she was and that every boy with a pulse at Berkley probably had a crush on her. "Somehow I think you'll manage," she replied.

Blair shook her head. "It's not right. You're going to miss everything. Why did your parents change their minds?"

Nikki briefly considered the scurvy excuse. "Does it really matter *why*?" she said instead, which, she had to admit, came out sounding rather mysterious and cool.

"I guess not." Blair sighed and sagged her shoulders. "This is *so* unfair. Maybe I could talk to them." She brightened. "You know how good I am with the guilt."

This was true, but Nikki knew better than to pull the manipulation tactic on her parents. "No, thanks. It'll only make things worse, believe me."

Blair twisted her ponytail around the fingers of her right hand. "I don't even want to go without you, but Mother's expecting me. I'll bet she makes me hang out with my cousin, Muffy, all summer now that you won't be around," she added with a slight pout. "She doesn't like to subject strangers to the torment, but she has no problem making *me* suffer through it."

Blair had a tendency toward the dramatic, but Nikki zeroed in on the cousin's name. "Tell me you're kidding. Your cousin's name is *not* Muffy!" She laughed.

Blair laughed, too. "No, no. Not really," she admitted. "It's just my personal nickname for her."

"Oh?" Nikki asked. "Do I want to know *why*?"

"See for yourself," Blair remarked and nodded down the pier.

As if on cue, a girl about their age with curly blond highlights twisted into a bun on the top of her head bounced down the planks, her baby pink tennis skirt flicking from side to side. "Oh, hi-yeeee, Blair!" Muffy cried, waving.

Nikki watched Blair's cousin quickly buzz in and around the crowd like a hyperactive bee as she made her way toward them. Blair was so casual and easygoing, it was hard to believe the two were even related. "She's definitely *energetic*."

Blair replied by heaving another sigh just as Muffy reached them.

"Hi, girls!" Muffy sang. "Hope you've been practicing your tennis if you want to win a game this summer, Blair." She put her hands together and did a little mock swing, then gave Nikki a friendly wink.

Blair plastered a fake smile onto her lips. "Sure have, cuz."

"*Awesome!*" Muffy said enthusiastically. "Well, I guess I'll beat you to the window seat. See you on the boat! Byeeeee!"

"She's soooo hyper," Blair complained. "I think I need a nap."

"I feel for you," Nikki said, watching as Muffy bounced and chatted her way to the boat. "But I still don't get why you call her . . ." And then, as

Blair's cousin turned to step onto the ship's entrance ramp, Nikki noticed it. From the back the bun kind of made the poor girl's head resemble a gigantic banana-walnut muffin. "Ahhh, I see. . . . Shouldn't you say something to her? I mean, she *is* your cousin."

"I've tried," Blair admitted. "But apparently the Muffstress saw the hairstyle during Fashion Week in New York and is convinced that I just don't want her to look good." She rolled her eyes. "And don't let that bubbly exterior fool you. The girl is completely fake. And seriously competitive. About everything. Ugh! This summer is going to reek!"

"Tell me about it," Nikki added, thinking back to her brothers and how they'd pretty much turned teasing her into a team sport.

The ferry horn sounded and Mr. Oliveri, a weathered deckhand who lived around the corner from Nikki, shouted, "All aboard! All aboard to Bella Island!"

As the crowd of polo-shirted men and women in straw hats pressed forward on the entrance ramp, Blair gave Nikki a big squeeze. "I'm going to miss you so much!"

"Me, too." Nikki hugged her back. She really

was. "Promise to call or text me as soon as anything juicy happens?"

"Totally," Blair said, racing up the ramp and boarding the boat just in time. "You, too, okay?" she called. "See ya!"

Nikki nodded and waved as she watched the jitney start its two-hour journey across to Bella Island. She stood there long enough for the pier to clear out and the din to fade except for the squawking of a few stray pelicans circling above the water, looking for breakfast. *Now what?* she wondered.

She must have seemed pretty pathetic standing there by herself because old Mr. Oliveri came over to console her.

"Don't worry, kid," he said, patting her shoulder. "Bella Island is only a ferry ride away." But to Nikki, that ride might as well have been a transatlantic cruise.

chapter 2

As the Bella Island ferry grew smaller and smaller on the horizon, Nikki knew she couldn't put off the confrontation with her parents forever. Then again, now that they'd all had some time to cool off, maybe she could *reason* with Mom and Dad. Maybe she could get them to change their minds again and to let her catch the next boat out of there. Okay, so it was doubtful, but hey, the least she could do was give it a shot.

Nikki strode back up the pier toward the Pelican Island Bridge and passed a group of retired fishermen chatting as they cast crabbing cages off the side rail. Just as she came upon the Bella Island ticket booth, she heard a burst of female laughter.

"Oh my God. Tommy is so hot!" a girl cried out.

Nikki slowed her pace, immediately recognizing the voice of her former best friend, Hannah

11

McVeigh. She stole a glance into the booth for confirmation. Uh-huh. Hannah's dark hair was cut into a funky bob — a lot shorter than Nikki remembered it being — but it was definitely Hannah. She was leaning on a counter, cooing over a picture (of Tommy, Nikki assumed) as her newish pals from P.I. High, Stephanie Saunders and Margaret something-or-other, looked on. Nikki guessed that they'd all gotten summer jobs at the ticket booth and it seemed as if they were having a blast together.

What felt like a gooey lump of pizza dough swiftly lodged itself into Nikki's throat. She knew she shouldn't let it get to her after all this time, but still, she and Hannah had been almost sisters since the first day of kindergarten — when they both arrived in Miss Gratenger's class wearing the same ugly purple plaid dress. They'd played on the monkey bars together, leaned on each other when their homes felt too crowded, giggled about first crushes.

Then, at the end of eighth grade, Nikki won an academic scholarship to Richfield Academy and, shortly after freshman year rolled around, Nikki's friendship with Hannah was dead. Done. *Finito*. The truly sad thing about the whole scenario was that, although Nikki had had her suspicions, she didn't *really* know what horrible thing she'd done to make Hannah and the rest of Nikki's old school crowd cut her off. Like a bad breakup, it was never explained. It just sort of *happened*. And now . . .

"*What* is she looking at?" Stephanie asked loudly from across the pier.

Nikki gulped, realizing that her inconspicuous glance had kind of turned into a stare.

Hannah tore herself away from the picture, glanced at Nikki, and shrugged. Then Margaret spat out, "What's your problem, Devita?"

"Um, nothing," Nikki mumbled. The sound of mean laughter stung as Nikki made a quick left and crossed back onto Pelican Island. *Great. The summer is finally looking up,* she thought sarcastically. Maybe she *should* have taken Blair up on her offer to guilt-trip the parents.

A few blocks later she found herself in front of the Italian Scallion, the Devita family's deli and catering service. The bell above the front entrance tinkled as she pushed open the lace-curtained door and stepped inside. Her dad had his favorite *Swingin' to the Oldies* CD crooning out of the stereo speakers, as usual.

Vince was already working behind the glass

counter, slicing up meats and filling catered lunch orders, while Paul chalked the daily specials onto a giant blackboard hanging on the wall.

Vito Devita turned from preparing the old-fashioned cart that housed several different varieties of olives, which could be had for $3.99 per pound. "Eh, there she is!" he said with his thick Italian accent. He opened his burly arms as he bopped to the beat of a Frank Sinatra tune. "What? You're not gonna give your papa a kiss?"

Nicole maneuvered around a towering biscotti display to plant a peck on his chubby cheek. "Sorry for blowing up at you and Mom this morning," she said.

"We know," he said, adjusting the long stained apron that stretched across his belly. "You're in high school now. You just wanna be with your friends."

His tone surprised Nikki. It was softer than it'd been earlier. Understanding, almost. The perfect in for her plea. "Speaking of which —" she began.

"Colie?" Mom appeared in the doorway that led to the kitchen. Petite and thin, Stella Devita clicked around the deli counter in her usual uniform, high heels and tiny mini. This one was leopard print. Mom had a great body, not to

14

mention *awesome* legs, but sometimes Nikki wondered if maybe there ought to be a law against a forty-five-year-old woman buying her wardrobe at Wet Seal.

"Hey, Mom," Nikki said.

"Let's sit down, honey." Mom led the way to the small table by the bay window where most of the major family discussions were had. "Your father and I need to talk to you about something. All right, baby doll?"

Uh-oh. She sounded serious . . . and *nice*, which was unusual for Nikki's no-nonsense mom. Maybe this wasn't about the morning's argument. "Is Grandma okay?" she asked cautiously.

"Of course. Your grandma's fine," Dad replied, then turned to Nikki's mother. "Do you want to tell her or should I?"

"Tell me what?" Nikki asked, looking back and forth from parent to parent. What was this all about?

"Well, your father and I know how disappointed you were about Bella Island, and we know that you're getting older and wanting to do new things —"

"*Fun* things," Nikki's father cut in.

Fun? Nikki broke into a grin, getting the hint.

Her parents had actually discovered the error of their ways and had decided to let her go to Bella — no reasoning (or pleading) required! Her heart thudded in anticipation as she wondered which bikini she'd wear to the beach first. The barely-there black string or the blue halter with the boy shorts? *"Go on,"* she said, prodding them to get it out so she could run home and grab her duffel bag.

"Well, what could be more fun than to work with your mama and papa at the store?" Dad asked, grinning, too. "Am I right?"

Wait. What? No! Nikki thought. Was this some kind of joke? She glanced around the shop, hoping that Paul and Vince were trying to punk her with the new video camera. Unfortunately Paul was now busy cleaning the espresso machine and Vince was shoving a wad of American cheese into his mouth.

"We knew you'd be surprised," Dad went on. "Your brothers didn't start until they were sixteen, but we think you're ready." He turned to Mom. "Right, Stella?"

"You bet," Mom replied, nodding. "You'll get minimum wage to start, just like your brothers did."

Nikki opened her mouth to protest, then snapped it shut. What was she supposed to say? *Uh, sorry, folks, slicing salami may be fun for you guys, but it isn't exactly my idea of a good time*? No, she didn't have the heart for it . . . *and* she wanted to live to see sixteen.

"Besides," Mom added with a knowing look in Nikki's direction. "Since you won't be spending the summer on Bella Island with Blair we thought you'd want to keep busy," which, translated into mother-daughter speak, meant: *Don't even think about bringing up Bella Island again, and you'll be working here so we can keep an eye on you 24/7.*

It's a done deal, Nikki thought bitterly. *So much for reasoning.*

Dad rubbed his hands together, then circled one arm around Nikki and the other around Mom. "I'm so glad we have the whole family working together; what a fantastic summer it will be, no?"

Both parents were beaming proudly now, as if starting work at the deli was some sort of weird passage into womanhood, and there was nothing Nikki could do except to say, "I can't wait to start."

"Yeah, it's Nicole, Colie, the Colirator . . . slicin' *turkey* . . . makin' a *sannndwich* . . . Collllllllle,"

Vince said the next day, grabbing a stack of paper cups from a cabinet while Nikki moved a slab of honey-roasted meat through a spinning cold-cut slicer.

"*You* are a dork," Nikki said, grinning and pointing a plastic-gloved finger at her brother as he crossed to the coffee counter. "Actually, this isn't so hard," she told Paul, who was supervising her push and pull the turkey along the blade. Perfect circles of paper-thin meat slipped out from the bottom of the machine. "I could do it with my eyes closed. See?" She shut them and continued slicing.

"Come on, Colie, cut it out," Paul warned her.

Nikki opened her eyes. "That's funny. *Cut it?* Get it? Isn't that what I'm doing?" She laughed at her own sorry excuse for a joke. Then she felt the blade nick her index finger. "Owww!" She swiped her hand away and the meat bounced onto the tiled floor.

"Geez!" Paul pulled her to a nearby sink and snapped off her gloves. "I *told* you to be careful," he said, running cool water over her fingers.

She winced as she watched pink liquid circle down the drain. Vince ran over with a bottle of disinfectant. He immediately sprayed down the machine and the stainless steel counter.

"What happened?" Dad came running out from the kitchen holding a spatula, his apron covered in tomato sauce.

"Nikki had a little accident," Paul reported. He inspected her fingers. "She's got a nice gash here. She's lucky. It could have been worse."

Nikki squirmed at the thought.

"Give me a break," Vince said, swiping up the turkey from the floor. "First she burns herself making steamed milk for Dad's cappuccino, then she cuts herself opening a can of crushed tomatoes. . . ."

"Don't forget the incident with the bleach," Paul added, gesturing to the white splash marks at the bottom of Vince's blue jeans.

"How could I?" Vince rolled his eyes. "I mean, come on, Colie. Didn't you grow up in this deli with the rest of us?"

Nikki blushed as she inspected the U-shaped cut on her wrist and the little burn mark right underneath the hem of her denim mini. It was all true. Every word. Granted, today she had a bit more responsibility than her "kid jobs" of stuffing napkin holders and filling the bagel bins, but when did she become such a klutzy freak?

Dad glanced at the clock hanging over the doorway to the kitchen. It was noon. "Colie, maybe you should take the rest of the day off."

"No, Dad," Nikki replied. "I want to make this work." Last night while unpacking her duffel she'd decided that she was really going to put forth an effort at the deli. After all, there was no use sulking about Bella Island anymore. She had to make the best of the situation. Besides, her parents were counting on her. "I'm all yours," she said, pressing a paper towel onto her wound. "Just as soon as I stop the bleeding."

Dad smiled. "That's my girl. She don't give up."

Nikki followed her father into the kitchen, where he was frying up a batch of chicken cutlets, then headed back to the office for the first aid kit.

"Again?" Mom asked when she saw Nikki rooting through the white metal box on top of a file cabinet. "Are you okay? Let me see."

"I'm fine," Nikki said. She plucked a bandage from the box and handed it to her mother. "Just not so good at cold cuts."

Mom stood from her desk in a short black skirt, a royal blue blouse with a three-inch-wide leather belt completing the outfit. "I'm sure we can find something for you to do," she said, wrapping Nikki's finger. "But it probably shouldn't involve sharp objects. Or hot things."

"Agreed," Nikki said, though that didn't leave many options.

"How's your math?" Mom asked. "Maybe you can help me with inventory and accounting."

"Okay, I guess," Nikki told her, but inside she was thinking, *Please, please, puh-leeze let there be something else for me to do.* Nikki had nothing against her mom, but she didn't want to spend the entire summer pushing a pencil in a cramped office.

"Hey, Pop!" Vince called. "We've got to get these deliveries out, but Paul needs help filling the other orders. What should I do?"

Yes! Nikki thought. "I can help!" she called, smoothing down her Italian Scallion T-shirt and looking to her mom for approval. Mom nodded, and Nikki ran up two steps and into the kitchen. "I'll do the deliveries, Dad."

"Good idea," he said, flipping a breaded cutlet. "You can use the new bike. Vince, you go help Paul."

"Why does *she* get the job with the tip

potential?" Vince asked, clearly disappointed. "Why can't she make sandwiches?"

"Because." Nikki playfully wiggled her bandaged finger under his nose. "*I* can't be trusted with a knife."

"Whatever." Vince pushed her hand out of the way and marched into the store, and Nikki went out back to grab the bike.

She found the three-speed silver cruiser in the tiny shed off the side of the store's gravel parking lot. A large white wicker basket lined with red-and-white cotton made the thing seem cute and girly. *Vince should probably thank me*, Nikki said to herself. *No way would he look cool in front of the ladies with this ride*. She hopped on and pulled it around front, where Paul was waiting with an armful of sandwiches, a list, and some small bills for change.

"The job is simple," he said. "You bring the sandwiches to the people and they pay you. But you've got to be fast. No more than twenty minutes a run. Got it?"

"Yup." Once the basket was filled with sandwiches Nicole was on her way. Luckily all of the deliveries were concentrated on the other side of the bridge, which was where the Scallion made most of its business.

Nikki glided over Pelican Island Bridge and zoomed past the jitney ticket booth as fast as her legs would pedal, hoping not to run into Hannah. She thought Richfield would have been dead with so many people off on Bella Island but that was far from the case. Although only staff mostly occupied the estates in the summertime, the town itself was flowing with tourists who came for the beautiful maritime museum as well as the local artists' galleries and antique stores dotting the main thoroughfare.

Nikki rode the bike onto the Main Street sidewalk, parking it in front of Gilded, a jewelry shop that specialized in expensive handmade pieces. She ran inside with a tomato-and-mozzarella with fresh basil on ciabatta, and a salami, provolone, and arugula wrap.

"Italian Scallion," she said, holding up the sandwiches.

A salesgirl handed her fourteen dollars. "Keep the change," she said with an intense stare, as if she were doing Nikki a huge favor.

Ooh. A whole thirty cents, Nikki thought.

"Thanks," she said on her way out. She found the next drop-off on her list and hopped back onto the bike.

This is great, Nikki thought as she pedaled down Main Street enjoying the fresh breeze sweeping in from the bay. *Much nicer than being stuck in Mom's office all day.* She lifted her face to take in the sunshine, glad to be outside, when her cell phone rang. She grasped for it in the bike's basket. "Hello?"

"Hey. It's Vince. Where are you?" her brother asked.

Nikki glided up a curb and onto the sidewalk. "On the way to my second delivery," she replied.

"That's *it*?" he said, as if she hadn't left the deli practically thirty seconds ago. "You should probably do better than that if you want to keep your job. Dad says that I can try deliveries if you're not fast enough. And the orders are piling up over here."

Nikki rolled her eyes. "Dream on, Vince. You're not getting my job . . . *or* my tips," she added, knowing it would bug him, and hung up. The money wasn't exactly worth fighting over but Vince didn't know that. And what was with him, anyway? she wondered, pedaling a bit faster. Why

24

was he being so annoying about this? It wasn't as if she'd ever be a huge help to Mom and Dad behind the counter like he was.

"Hey, look out!" someone yelled.

Huh? Nikki glanced up and spotted some unsuspecting boy about her age wearing an orange T-shirt and a baseball cap in her direct path. She swerved quickly to the left, just missing him. "Sorry!" she called back to him.

The boy removed his hat, exposing an extreme buzz cut. Even from this distance Nikki could see his striking blue eyes. They were big and round and surprised-looking. *Oh my God, he's so hot,* she thought, *and I almost killed him!*

He pointed in her direction. "Hey!"

"Sorry!" Nikki said again, mortified. *Could I feel like a bigger loser?* she wondered just as her front wheel skidded on a patch of wet pavement. A second later Nikki came crashing to the ground. Her skirt flapped up to her waist, exposing her peach-colored briefs with the hula-girl pattern that she *knew* she shouldn't have worn. Sandwiches scattered across the sidewalk in all directions.

Apparently, she could.

chapter 3

Red-faced, and with the surprising agility of a ninja, Nikki rolled to her feet in an instant, though she knew it was useless since the hot guy, along with the rest of Main Street, had seen the humiliating accident.

"You okay?" the boy asked, rushing over. "That was some fall."

"Me? Oh, I'm fine," Nikki said, tugging at her skirt. She tried to play it off by picking up the sandwiches as if nothing had happened — as if she hadn't, in fact, just flashed him her hula panties.

She spotted some mani-pedi ladies staring out the window of a nearby nail salon. "Move along. Nothing to see here," she said, flicking her hands at them, but the ladies kept staring. *Oh, God. Why is this happening to me?* she silently screamed.

"You sure you're okay?" the guy asked, inspecting a U-shaped cut on her arm.

26

"Oh, this?" Nikki glanced at it. "I had that before. I'm fine. Really. It probably looked worse than it was." She chuckled nervously.

The hottie gazed at her with what Nikki considered to be the bluest eyes on the planet, which happened to contrast with the dark stubble on his head. *Come on, think of something witty and clever to say to him,* Nikki told herself. "Ummmmmmm . . ."

Unable to come up with *anything*, let alone something flirty, she glanced away shyly as she finished gathering her stuff. She shoved the bundle of sandwiches into the basket and picked up her bike. It had a scratch or two on it, but nothing major.

"So, I guess you're delivering sandwiches," the guy piped up.

"Huh? Oh. Right. Uh-huh. Maybe you want to order one sometime. I'm sure there's a menu around here somewhere," Nikki replied, fully aware that she was now babbling. She began to search the pile of sandwiches and found a flyer at the bottom. As she tugged at it, a hoagie toppled out of the basket.

"Whoa!" The boy tried to catch it, but it fell to the sidewalk with a splat.

That was when Nikki noticed he was holding a leash, which was attached to a tiny orange Pomeranian, which now had a big yellowish-brown squirt of honey mustard matting the fur on top of its head.

The boy laughed. "Aunt Winnie is not going to be happy about that."

"Oops!" Nikki threw the leaky sandwich back into the bicycle basket, grabbed a pile of napkins, and attempted to wipe off the dog as it yapped and nipped at her fingers. "Sorry!"

"Forget it," the boy said, crouching down and taking the napkins from Nikki. As he did this he smiled and Nikki smiled back, feeling a weird and exciting energy ping back and forth between them. Her stomach suddenly felt as if a hundred butterflies had decided to get together for a game of tag in there.

"Well, I've got to get Button back to my aunt," the boy said, gesturing to the Pomeranian and turning to leave.

"Wait!" Nikki cried a little too loudly. She hoped that didn't come off as slightly psycho.

The boy turned back and Nikki handed him the menu. "You forgot this," she said. Then, in a bold move, she added, "My name's Nikki, by the way. What's yours?"

"Daniel," he said.

Not knowing what else to do, Nikki casually gazed back into the window of the nail salon, where the women inside seemed to have lost interest, thank *God*. She waited a few seconds to see if Daniel had anything to ask her. Like maybe if he could have her number or something.

Daniel sort of coughed and shoved his hands into the pockets of his enormous camouflage shorts.

Why isn't he asking? Nikki waited a few more seconds. *Maybe he's shy*, she told herself. *Maybe you should just ask* him *for* his *number*.

Why not? This *was* the twenty-first century, after all. Okay. She'd go for it. In three . . . two . . . one . . .

"Um, Daniel, I . . . I . . ." *I can't do it!* she thought, chickening out. "I guess I'd better finish my deliveries. . . ." She paused, giving him a chance to talk.

"Oh. Right. No problem," he said, walking backward. "It was really nice meeting you, Nikki." He tripped over Button's leash but recovered nicely. "Heh, heh." He grinned nervously and waved. "Bye, Nikki."

She liked the way he said her name a lot. "Bye." Nikki smiled again and waved as Daniel headed down Main Street with Button, really wishing she'd had the nerve to get his number. He was so adorable and sweet. She wouldn't mind seeing him again. No, she wouldn't mind it at all.

Two days later, the sky was blue and cloudless and the scent of sardines barely noticeable as Nikki pedaled her first deliveries toward the Pelican Island Bridge. Her phone rang to the tune of a spunky salsa beat and Nikki bobbed her head to a few bars as she checked out the screen. *Cool,* she thought, *a text from Blair.* She pulled to the side of the road to take a look.

helllllllllp! Muffy strks again! what up w/u?

Nikki laughed, imaging how Blair's annoying cousin was torturing her friend. She keyed a quick message with her news:

Met hot boy.

She pressed SEND and her phone rang almost instantly. She glanced at the screen. Blair, of course.

"What's his name? What does he look like? When are you going out?" Blair babbled as soon as Nikki picked up.

"It's Daniel. He's really cute in that shaved-head-alterna-boy kind of way, and I don't even know if he likes me yet. I'm on a quest to find out . . . and to get his digits. I'll keep you posted."

"You'd better," Blair said. "And I hope you're wearing that cute white mini that shows off your legs. That'll get his attention."

"You think?" Nikki asked, glancing down at that very skirt. She didn't want to admit that yesterday and today she'd put on extra-hot outfits hoping to run into Daniel. Needless to say, her mom had been happy to see Nikki in a skirt again, but now that Nikki had it on she wasn't so sure it was a good idea. And maybe she should have left the kitten-heeled slides in the closet, too, even if they were fabulous. Oh, well.

"Ugh, here comes Muffy with her tennis racquet," Blair whispered.

Nikki heard a scuffling sound, then a soft thud. "Where are you?" she asked.

"Towel hut," Blair whispered. "I can't play another game of tennis, Nik. We just got here and she's already wiped the court with me six — oh, gotta go!" *Click.*

Nikki almost felt sorry for Blair, but not quite. *At least things are looking up on my end,* she thought, flipping her phone shut and hopping back on the bike to begin her deliveries. She was bound to run into Daniel again sooner or later.

By the time she'd reached the end of her twelfth run without a single Daniel sighting, however, Nikki had resigned herself to the fact that it was probably going to happen later rather than sooner. As she pedaled across the bridge back to Pelican Island her mind raced with thoughts about the cute boy with the intense eyes.

She wondered who he was. A tourist? She'd never seen him before but then that didn't mean anything. She didn't know every guy in Richfield and/or the surrounding area. But then again, if he did live around here he'd probably be vacationing on Bella Island with everybody else.

Nikki glided to a halt in front of the Italian Scallion and parked the bike against the building. *So if Daniel's a tourist, that means he'll be leaving by the end of the summer, at the latest,* she said to herself.

She shook her head. *What are you doing, Nikki? You don't even know if he likes you and you're already stressing about when he's leaving?* She decided to think about the way he said her name instead. *Nikki, Nikki, Nikki . . .*

"You wanna talk to *who*?" Nikki heard Dad saying into the telephone when she entered the shop. "My daughter? Why? Who's this?"

Nikki gasped. She knew exactly who it was! Or at least she *hoped* she knew. It made sense now. Daniel didn't ask for her home number because she'd already given him her *work* number — on the menu! Clever guy. "I'll take it. It's my friend," she told her father, who handed over the phone, then disappeared in the kitchen. "Hello?" she said into the receiver.

"Uhhhh, is this Colie?" a boy's gruff voice said over the line.

"Daniel?" she asked, though now that she'd heard him she wasn't so sure. At the same time she wondered, *How does he know about Colie? He knows me only as Nikki.*

"Yeah, that's me," the guy breathed. "Want to go out tonight? I hear you're an awesome kisser."

Girls giggled in the background. "Shhh!" someone said through the laughter.

Now she knew it wasn't Daniel. "Who is this?" she demanded.

"You know," the guy said through a snicker. "Danny."

The girls cackled louder right before Nikki slammed the phone into its cradle on the wall. "What jerks!" she muttered.

Paul walked by with a case of soda on his shoulder. "Who's a jerk?"

Couldn't she have a second of privacy? "Nobody," Nikki replied, though she had a feeling she knew who was behind the prank call. With no Caller ID on the store phone, she picked up the receiver again and dialed *69 to see if she could find out who was playing with her. She jotted down the recorded number and then dialed it.

"Bella Island Jitney!" a girl answered with a singsongy tone. "How may I help you?"

Nikki slammed the phone again. "Jerks!"

"Who?!" Paul asked again, this time from the drink refrigerator.

"Nobody!" Nikki cried and stormed to the door of the shop. On the way out she heard Vince ask Paul, "What's her problem?"

Oh, Nikki had a problem, all right. Three of

them: Hannah, Stephanie, and Margaret. And she knew how the game went down. She couldn't just let this prank go unchecked.

Nikki marched across the bridge, heading straight for the jitney ticket booth. She tried to figure out what she was going to say along the way, but before she knew it she was there.

Stephanie's mouth dropped open when she saw Nikki approaching. She nudged Margaret, whose nose was buried in a fashion magazine. Behind them was a tall lanky boy with a ton of acne who, Nikki suspected, had been the one put up to make the call. *The mastermind must be in the back somewhere*, she thought as she approached the booth.

"Get Hannah out here," she demanded to no one in particular.

"Did somebody say something, Stephanie?" Margaret asked, flipping a page of her magazine.

"*I* did," Nikki replied, planting a hand on an article about how to get perfect abs. "Get Hannah," she repeated.

Hannah came walking up behind Nikki with a gigantic Big Gulp in hand — probably Mountain Dew, which was her drink of choice. She seemed surprised and annoyed that Nikki was there and shot her a dirty look. "What is *she* doing here?" Hannah asked her friends.

"As if you don't know," Nikki muttered. She turned to confront the girl. "Aren't you a little *old* for making prank phone calls, Hannah?"

"Huh? I don't even know what you're talking about," Hannah said.

"Give me a break. I traced it back to the jitney booth, and I know you made *him* do it for you." Nikki gestured to the boy with the acne. Hearing this, the boy slinked out of the booth into a back office.

"Don't flatter yourself," Hannah replied. "I wouldn't waste the quarter on you. And I just got here, anyway."

"Oh, *really*." Nikki gazed at Hannah to see if she was lying. The girl was wearing a pair of denim shorts and a navy halter. Her jitney polo shirt was slung over one shoulder, and she was seriously staring Nikki down without so much as a twitch of an eyelid. She *could* be telling the truth, Nikki surmised. Then she began to think that maybe coming there wasn't such a good idea, but there was no way to turn back now without looking like a complete idiot.

"Well, *some*body here pranked me." Nikki

focused on Stephanie and Margaret, who smirked at her.

"*So?*" Stephanie said, then proceeded to crack up.

Margaret seemed to find this funny, too, and giggled like a hyena.

And Hannah just stood there, which irritated Nikki even more than the phone call had. "Thanks a lot, Hannah. I'll bet you gave them my number," she said. "You know, I thought we were friends once."

"Whatever," Hannah said, rolling her eyes.

"Yeah, *whatever*," Nikki repeated. This wasn't getting her anywhere. She turned to storm off but accidentally twisted her left foot out of its kitten heel, knocking her off balance . . . and into an unsuspecting Hannah.

"Whoa!" Hannah squeezed her Big Gulp hard as she stumbled to the ground, popping off the lid and releasing a thick stream of Mountain Dew.

Nikki winced as the greenish-yellowy liquid arced a path toward the jitney booth, then soaked the counter along with everything on top of it and everyone behind it. Stephanie and Margaret squealed in horror, resulting in an angry manager emerging from the office.

"Sorry, Mr. Harris!" Hannah said, rushing to the booth, which, Nikki believed, was her cue to cut out of there.

She made a quick pivot and headed to the bridge. When she reached it she looked back at the ticket booth. Mr. Harris was now waving his arms angrily as he reprimanded the girls, and Nikki kind of felt bad for them. She didn't want them to get into trouble at work, just not to call her anymore.

By the time Nikki arrived back at the deli she was mentally exhausted. It had been a tough day and she couldn't wait to go home and crawl underneath her bedspread.

"Oh, wait a sec," Paul was saying over the sound of Dean Martin singing "That's Amore." "She's right here. Hold on." He held out the phone to her. "It's for you. Some guy. Says he's a friend of yours?"

Nikki felt an angry fire well up inside of her. After all that, she could not *believe* Stephanie and Margaret had the nerve to make that guy prank her again! They must be having a big laugh right about now.

She grabbed the phone from her brother.

"You'd better not call me at this number again, buck-o!" she shouted into the phone.

"Buck-o?" Paul walked away, snickering.

"Um, Nikki?" the boy said. "Sorry. I — I didn't know you'd be mad about it."

Nikki gulped, her stomach fluttering into knots, because this time she recognized the voice. "Daniel?" she asked. "Is that you?"

chapter 4

Nikki gripped the phone tightly to her ear. "Sorry I bothered you," she heard Daniel say. "I'll go."

"No, wait. Don't hang up," Nikki quickly replied. "I thought you were somebody else." She leaned against the deli counter and pushed back some stray hairs that had slipped out of her ponytail. "So, um, what's up?" she said, trying to sound normal. Inside she was freaking out. *He called me! He actually called me! I can't believe he called me!* she thought over and over.

"So, do you want to go?" Daniel was asking.

"Huh?" She must have missed it. "Go where?"

"For a walk," Daniel said. "My aunt wants Button to get some exercise and I don't really know where to take her. Do you?"

"Sure. There's a nice dog run in Richfield Park," Nikki told him. "I'm just about finished with work. I'll run home and get my dog, too. Okay?"

"Great," Daniel said. "How about we meet by

40

that bridge in, like, fifteen? You know, the one with those bird statues on it."

Nikki would rather they didn't, but she also didn't want to get into the whole my-new-worst-enemy-works-near-there-and-I-don't-want-her-and-her-nosy-friends-to-see-me-meeting-up-with-a-cute-boy thing. So she said, "Okay. See you then!"

She hung up the phone and sighed, barely able to process the fact that she'd just made a date with hot Daniel. Then she wondered if she could call dog-walking an *official* date or if it was considered only hanging out. Oh, well. No time to work out the intricacies. She had only minutes to get ready! She called to Mom and Dad, telling them that she was going home.

"Was that the jerk you were talking to?" Paul stopped her on the way out.

"Who?" Nikki asked.

"You know. The guy on the phone. *Buck-o!*" He laughed and poked her in the arm. "So when are we going to meet this Buck-o guy, huh?"

Vince trotted in through the front door, holding a box of paper napkins with ITALIAN SCALLION printed on them. "Who's Bucky?" he asked. "Some kid with a bad overbite?" He laughed at his own joke.

41

Not that Nikki had had a lot of boyfriends — okay, not that she'd had *any* — but if she had, *this* would be the reason why she would *never* have brought any of them around the house. "Shut up," she told her brothers, and left.

As soon as Nikki got home, she raced up the stairs to her room and tore apart her closet for the perfect outfit: something that said playful and casual, yet sophisticated and sexy. Three changes, four ponytail redoes, and one armpit sniff test later, Nikki had decided on a pair of cute denim capris, a whitewashed khaki graphic tee, and letting her natural brown waves fall to her shoulders. A spritz of body splash and a swipe of strawberry lip gloss and Nikki was out the door.

"Oops! I need a dog." She ran back inside and grabbed the leash that was hanging on a hook in the foyer. "Rocky!" She found him snoozing underneath the kitchen table, and shook the leash. "Come on, boy. Let's go for a walk."

Rocky opened his eyes, then closed them again. Apparently he wasn't in the mood.

"You're coming with me whether you like it or not," she said, crawling underneath the table and snapping the leash onto Rocky's collar. "Let's move it, puppy!"

It took a few tugs of the leash before Rocky cooperated and trotted alongside her to the bridge.

Still on the Pelican Island side, she spotted Daniel standing at the opposite end with his back to her, clearly expecting her to be coming from the other direction. She liked the look he was going for with a simple T-shirt and baggy shorts with a long, thin chain hanging from a belt loop and disappearing in his side pocket, probably attached to his wallet.

"Hey," she said, coming up behind him with Rocky in tow.

Daniel turned, and Nikki wondered if she should greet him with a kiss on the cheek or a handshake or what. She settled on a safe little wave.

"Hey, Nikki." He was holding the fluffy little Pomeranian in his left hand. A pink bow was tied at the top of Button's head to keep the orange fur out of her eyes.

Nikki glanced at Rocky, all gray and shaggy and slobbering on her right foot. "Ew. Rocky!"

Daniel smiled as he tilted his head. "Your dog's name is *Rocky*? And you work at a place called the *Italian Scallion*?"

Nikki shrugged. "My dad's kind of obsessed

with Sylvester Stallone. I'm just lucky my mom stopped him from naming me Adrian," she added with a slight shiver. "Now, that would have been *really* weird. Can you imagine me as a kid, playing with my friends, and having my dad call me to come home?" She framed her mouth with her hands and imitated the main character in *Rocky I, II, III,* and *IV, "Adriaaaaan!"*

Daniel laughed. "You're pretty funny. Actually, pretty *and* funny," he added.

So, he thinks I'm pretty, Nikki thought, feeling her stomach do an excited flip. *This is good.* "You're pretty *corny*," she said, playing it cool and teasing him a little. "I like that in a guy."

"Good," Daniel said with a friendly grin. "Hey, I didn't know you were from the island," he said, gesturing to the two stone pelicans hovering over the center of the bridge. "I've never been over there. Should we take the dogs that way?"

"I don't know." Nikki hesitated for two reasons. 1) Everything was way nicer in Richfield than on Pelican, and 2) if her family saw her with Daniel she'd surely have to answer a ton of questions about him. And it was kind of nice to have something all to herself for once — at least for a little while, anyway. "The dog run in Richfield is *so* awesome," she hinted. "We don't even *have* one on Pelican. I usually take Rocky to this tiny run-down beach."

"The beach? Cool!" He seemed so excited about it.

"It's not an actual *beach*, per se. Only a little sand, really," Nikki said, hoping to discourage him, but it wasn't happening.

Daniel was already walking toward her side of the bridge. He stopped to place Button on the ground and the dog immediately whined until she was picked up again.

Oh, well. Just go with it, Nikki told herself and stepped beside him. "Your aunt's dog isn't much of a walker, is she?" she asked, glancing at the fluffy pup in his arms.

Daniel smiled. "Not really. Button here spends most of her day hanging out in a pink tote bag." He scratched behind the dog's perky ears. "I would have brought it along, but it didn't go with my outfit."

Nikki laughed and let Rocky run ahead of them but reined him in when they reached the edge of the bridge. She'd decided to take a different route to the beach so they wouldn't have to pass by the deli.

"I told you, it's not much," Nikki said, when they'd arrived. Scattered driftwood and hollow horseshoe-crab shells dotted the dark pebbly sand. A couple of old rotted piers, minus their walkways, jutted into the sea. She unclipped Rocky's leash and let him go for a run at the water's edge.

Daniel set Button on her feet. She seemed afraid to move at first, but eventually trotted through the sand after Rocky with her head and tail held high.

Nikki perched on a large piece of wood and watched the dogs play. "So, what do you think of my little island?" she asked just as the sea air blew a gust of fish scent up from the ocean.

"It's, um, *fragrant*," he admitted and sat next to her.

"Tell me about it." Nikki wrinkled her nose. "There's a lot of fishing going on around the island. See that?" She pointed up at a flock of four pelicans swirling above the water. The large gray-and-white birds circled one, two, three times before nose-diving, kamikaze style, into the water, then emerging one by one with fresh silver fish in their beaks.

"Wow, that's —" Daniel said.

Nikki raised a hand to stop him, then pointed. "Wait for it. . . ."

A moment later a half-eaten fish suddenly plopped out of the sky and onto the wet sand just out of reach of the lapping sea. Then, seemingly out of nowhere, ten to twenty tiny white birds scurried across the sand to peck on the leftovers.

"Whoa. It's, like, so *Discovery Channel* out here," Daniel said, staring at the scene.

"Yeah," Nikki agreed. "Who needs cable when you've got all this?" Feeling a bit more comfortable, she leaned back, propping her elbows in the sand and letting her legs hang over the driftwood.

Rocky was now being chased by a yapping Button and headed this way. "Rowwwwlf!" he barked, and jumped into Daniel's arms, tackling him into the sand.

"Hey!" Daniel laughed, and petted the sandy and slobbering Rocky until the dog was satisfied, while Button continued to yap and yap.

"I think Rocky likes you." Nikki tried hard not to giggle as Daniel sat up, brushing sand from his head and shirt. When he was finished he leaned back next to Nikki and Rocky trotted around to sit on her other side.

That's a boy, Rocky. Good work, she thought,

ruffling the shaggy fur on her dog's head. Then she turned to Daniel. With his body only inches from hers, she wondered if he could hear the thumping of her heart. She also wondered if maybe she shouldn't have passed on the gum after eating that egg-salad sandwich for lunch.

Daniel rolled onto his side, facing her, and said, "I like being here with you, despite the stench."

"By *stench* you mean the fish, right?" she asked. *Tell me I didn't just say that out loud*, she silently prayed. Judging by Daniel's amusement, however, she knew that she had.

"You're hilarious," he said, cracking up.

Nikki decided to hold off on the jokes for a little while in the interest of information-gathering. "So, what's your story?" she asked him. "What brings you to lovely Richfield?"

Daniel shrugged. "My parents are sailing around the world on their yacht and I'm staying with my aunt until school starts up again."

Nikki doubled over in laughter. "No, seriously," she said, trying to stop herself.

"Seriously," Daniel said. He didn't seem to be joking.

"Seriously?" she asked, just to be sure.

Daniel nodded. "They've been gone, so far . . ."

He looked to the sky as if he were trying to remember. "Three and a half months."

"So, they trust you enough to stay home alone?" she asked, barely able to comprehend it. Pretty much the only time Nikki was alone was when she was in the bathroom, and even then it wasn't long before somebody was pounding on the door to get in.

"Not exactly," Daniel responded. "I go to a military school in Parkchester, two towns away." He brushed a hand over his buzzed head. "Haven't you noticed my extreme haircut?"

"Uh-huh, very nice," Nikki commented. "I just thought you were, you know, alternative or something." She squinted, trying to visualize Daniel looking totally cute in his dress blues. Suddenly a barrage of questions popped into her head, such as: Why was he going to military school? Did he miss his parents? Where did his aunt live? Did he like Nikki as much as she liked him? Did he want to go out on a date *without* the dogs? But she started with the basics. "Any brothers or sisters?" she asked.

"Nope. Just me," Daniel said. "How about you? What's your family like?"

Nikki let out an exasperated sigh. "I've got two

older brothers. Twins. Vince and Paul. They drive me *crazy*! My parents, you already know, own the Scallion, and we all work there. I'm the delivery girl extraordinaire."

"Sounds fun," Daniel said.

"It's okay." Nikki paused. "I was supposed to go to Bella Island for the summer but my plans changed at the last minute." She wasn't sure why she added that last little tidbit. Maybe it was because with parents who circled the world by sea, Daniel clearly had a more interesting and glamorous life than she did.

Daniel nodded knowingly. "Yeah. Aunt Winnie's been trying to get me to chill over there, make some friends, but it's just not my scene, you know? Besides, who would keep my aunt and this little one company?"

Nikki watched him gently stroke Button, who had now wedged herself into the crook of his arm and was snoring softly. "Awww. She's sweet."

Daniel looked up, his eyes meeting Nikki's, and she felt that familiar electricity gently prick her skin as it zinged between them. She tried to think of some funny and memorable thing to say but couldn't, so she gazed toward the sea instead.

"Nikki, I'm really glad you didn't go to Bella Island," she heard Daniel say after a while. "Otherwise we never would have met."

Nikki felt her cheeks grow rosy, not because she was feeling weird or embarrassed or anything but because, at that very moment, she was thinking exactly the same thing.

chapter 5

"I'm telling you, Pop. It's too much," Paul said at the family's table in the store the next morning as Ella Fitzgerald and Louis Armstrong crooned to each other in the background. "Between the walk-ins and the call-ins Vince and I can't handle it alone — even with Nikki making all the deliveries."

"Yeah," Vince agreed just as he was about to bite into a huge cannoli.

"You can't have pastries for breakfast," Mom said, joining them at the table. She swiped the cannoli out of Vince's hand and replaced it with peppers and eggs on a roll. "Eat this. You need the protein," she said and sat next to Nikki.

Nikki took a sip of grapefruit juice and nibbled on her English muffin as she listened to her family contemplate hiring another employee. Only a few days in and she could already see the problem. Business had been growing steadily ever since the Italian Scallion appeared as a "must do" in a popular New England magazine last spring. Now that the summer and the tourists were here, it was getting harder and harder to keep things under control.

"We'll put an ad in the paper tomorrow," Mom said, "and a HELP WANTED sign in the window. I'm sure one of the local kids needs a job."

Dad nodded. "I just wish we could get someone from the family. What about your second cousin, Angela?" he asked Mom. "She has a daughter, don't she?"

"Yes, but Lauren is eight, dear," Mom replied.

"Oh." Dad tapped his chin with a finger. "Who else can we think of?"

It was about then when Nikki lost interest in the conversation at hand. Her mind drifted back to the awesome time she'd had hanging out with Daniel on the beach yesterday and how his piercing eyes had seemed to drink in her every word. They'd discussed a million and four topics ranging from their favorite subjects in school to how they both loved pepperoni and black olives on their pizza but were completely opposed to anchovies, to their debate on whether or not pro wrestling could be considered a real sport, considering it was totally scripted. Nikki didn't think so, but Daniel pointed out that getting body-slammed by a two-hundred-fifty-pound guy in a Speedo has got to hurt, even if you know it's coming.

Then Nikki had received a call from Mom, wondering where she was, and Nikki and Rocky had to head back home for supper. Before parting, she and Daniel exchanged cell numbers and e-mail addresses and had made plans to meet with their Rollerblades today at the war memorial park on Pelican Island. Nikki couldn't wait to see him again.

Her deliveries went by in a blur, so much so that she was surprised to find that by the end of the day she had made twenty-five dollars in tips!

On the way home Nikki shot Daniel a quick text:

Be there in ten!

She found her old Rollerblades in the back of her closet, next to a baton and a green glittery mermaid costume she'd worn marching in her first — and last — Bait 'n' Tackle festival parade when she was twelve. The festival occurred every summer, but Nikki had decided that wearing a mermaid costume once in a lifetime was enough for anybody's memory book. In fact, she kind of wanted to forget about it, but unfortunately her parents had stored the moment in time in their video camera.

Nikki pushed aside the costume, grabbed her skates, dusted them off, and threw them in a backpack before heading out. She found Daniel sitting on the edge of the center fountain, all skated up and ready to go. He waved when he saw Nikki approach.

"Don't say I didn't warn you," he said as she sat next to him and pulled on her Rollerblades. "I haven't done this in a while."

"Me neither. We'll go slow." She popped her sneakers into her pack and slipped it over her shoulders. "Ready?"

"Yup." Daniel stood gingerly, taking her hand, and the two of them pushed off on the pavement.

Good thing I'm wearing wrist guards, Nikki thought, well aware of her increasingly sweaty palms squishing around underneath them. It didn't take long for Nikki to notice that Daniel was an awesome blader. He flipped easily between skating backward and forward along the path around the park while Nikki concentrated on staying upright as they chatted about music and their favorite bands.

"A couple of buds and I thought we were so cool for listening to all this old stuff," Daniel was saying. "We even started our own rap group called Beastieface. Kind of like an homage to old-school Beastie Boys."

"Before or after they went all Tibetan Buddhist?" Nikki asked.

Daniel spun in front of her so that they were face-to-face. "Wait. You like the Beastie Boys, too?" he asked, impressed.

"Totally," Nikki said, nodding. "I'm into all kinds of music. Well, except for Ashlee Simpson. I don't know, maybe I'm allergic."

"I hear that," Daniel said, flipping forward again as they began an incline.

When the two of them reached the apex, Nikki stopped and gazed at the winding slope falling down the other side. She looked back the way they had come, which was almost as steep. *Now I remember why these things were catching dust in the back of my closet*, she thought, kind of hoping that Daniel would suggest they take off their skates and walk down.

"That's a nice ride," Daniel said, clearly itching to go.

Nikki could hardly wimp out now. She'd just have to fake it. "Last one down to the bottom is a Beastieface," she said playfully before pushing off and going for it.

You can do this, she thought as she rolled along the pavement faster and faster. *Don't be afraid of the speed . . . just* — "Whoa!" She flapped out her arms, adjusting for a sudden balance issue. Then, gaining momentum and a little confidence, she crouched her upper body like a slalom skier and went even faster. "Yeahhhhhhhhh!" she yelled, actually enjoying herself for a second. But before she knew it, her ankles were shaking from the speed and she was losing control. "Ahhhhhhhh!"

"Brake! Use your brake!" Daniel called from somewhere behind her.

Nikki tried to push her left leg forward but instead of stopping, she totally wiped out. She dove for the grassy meadow to her right. Unfortunately it wasn't as soft as it looked. "Ungf!"

"Nikki!" Daniel swirled down the path after her, cutting a right at the meadow. He tripped when his wheels met the grass, and he landed face-first at Nikki's feet. "Ungf!"

"You okay?" she asked.

He rolled onto his back and looked at her. "Yeah. You?"

"Yeah," Nikki said, sitting up and rubbing her elbow. Then she fell back onto the grass and propped her left skate on her right knee — too hard. "Ow!"

Daniel cracked up.

"Hey, no laughing!" Nikki said, swatting him lightly on the arm. "I feel silly enough for wiping out like that."

"At least you did it with style," Daniel commented. "Seriously. You were, like, in warp speed going down that hill."

Daniel's eyes sparkled as he grinned at her, and Nikki found herself wanting to touch his face with her hand . . . wanting to know what it felt like to kiss him. "I guess I was," she whispered.

He leaned in a little closer and gently brushed a piece of grass from her hair.

Does he *want to kiss* me? Nikki wondered. The excited butterflies seemed to escape from her belly and flutter down her arms and legs. She hoped that he did.

"Hey, want to get some ice cream?" Daniel

asked, pulling away. "I saw a Mr. Freezie truck by the park's entrance." He rolled into a sitting position and flicked off the wheels of his skates, leaving him wearing a pair of cool-looking boots.

"Sure," Nikki replied, a little disappointed. Could it be that Daniel just didn't like her like that? Or maybe he didn't feel as if it was the right *place* for a first kiss?

She glanced around. The park wasn't crowded, by any means, but there *was* the occasional bike rider flying down the path and a group of about six kids were kicking around a soccer ball on the other side of the meadow.

Or maybe he really *did* have a sudden uncontrollable desire for soft-serve. Nikki could relate. She was sometimes that way when it came to peanut-butter-and-Nutella sandwiches.

Daniel grasped Nikki's hand to help her up and held on to it all the way to the park's entrance. His hand felt a little clammier than hers, but strong, and Nikki decided to forget about what the whole hand-holding thing might mean and to just enjoy it.

It seemed as though they were the only teenagers waiting in the Mr. Freezie line but Nikki and

Daniel didn't care. With ice cream in hand, they sat on a low wall slurping on their cones and enjoying the early evening sun.

"This park is pretty nice," Daniel commented, and Nikki had to agree.

"I never really think of coming here," she admitted. "Usually my friends and I just hang out in Richfield."

"It's a great place for people-watching," Daniel added, which was also true. From where they were sitting they could see across the Pelican Island Bridge and watch a light crowd of pass-ersby in every shape and size.

Nikki guessed that the strollers by the pier were tourists, while the more hurried people were clearly on their way home from work. A girl with short dark hair seemed to be in a super rush, weaving in and out of the crowd, then marching purposefully across the bridge.

Nikki groaned when she realized that the girl was Hannah, and that she was almost right on top of them. She hid her face behind Daniel's shoulder until Hannah had passed. "All clear?" she asked.

"Hiding from someone?" Daniel asked. "Who was that?"

"Just some girl," Nikki started, but then thought that if things went well with Daniel the story would probably have to come out sometime. "We used to be friends, that is, until I got a scholarship to Richfield Academy for Girls. Now she, like, totally hates me for some unknown reason."

"You got a *scholarship* to the Academy?" Daniel asked, amazed. "Wow, you must be a superbrain," he said.

Nikki wasn't sure if he was impressed or turned off by her smarts. "It's no big deal," she said, wanting to change the subject.

"Yes, it is," Daniel went on. He leaned in and gave her a nudge. "I'm impressed."

Cool! "Thanks," Nikki said. "So how come you know so much about the Academy?" she asked, curious.

"I guess I know a few people who go there," Daniel said with a shrug.

"Really?" Nikki said. She was just about to ask, "Who?" when the theme song to *Rocky* jingled in her backpack.

"Let me guess," Daniel said with a laugh. "Your dad?"

"The one and only." Nikki reached into her bag and felt for her phone. She found it underneath her skates and pulled it out just before the music was about to end. "Hey, Dad," she said, answering it.

"Colie, your mama wanted me to remind you. Come by the store in ten minutes. Give us a hand with closing. Okay?" Dad asked.

"No problem, Dad," Nikki said. "See you in a few." She flipped the phone shut.

"I guess that means you have to go," Daniel said.

Nikki nodded. "But we can pick up where we left off tomorrow, if you want." She took one final lick of her cone, then dumped the rest in a nearby pail.

"Can't," Daniel admitted. "I've got stuff, but how about Saturday? We can do something a little different, you know?"

"Oh?" Nikki raised her eyebrows.

Daniel held up his hands in defense. "No rolling on a bunch of tiny wheels, though, I *swear.*"

"Good." Nikki stood there for a moment, waiting for his cue on the good-bye. She didn't know if she should casually lean in and kiss him on the cheek or give him a friendly hug or a handshake or another wave. . . .

Still no cue . . .

"Well, um, I guess I'll go now," she said, hoping he'd get the hint.

"Right." Daniel shoved the rest of the cone in his mouth and stood. "I should probably go home, too," he mumbled through a full mouth. "See you Saturday." He gave her a friendly little punch on the arm, then turned to cross the bridge. "I'll call you."

"Later." Nikki turned in the opposite direction and headed to the store, a bit confused by Daniel's gesture. *A punch?* As far as taps on the arm were concerned, Nikki had no idea if Daniel's was meant to say: "Sorry, just a friend," or "I really like you but I'm trying to be cool about it." *Well, at least it was some sort of body contact,* she thought. *That's got to be good, right?*

When she arrived at the Scallion, Nikki found her father humming along to an ancient Frank Sinatra tune on the stereo as he scrubbed down a stainless steel counter.

"You're in a cheery mood, Dad." Nikki picked up a sponge and some Windex and started spraying down the outside of a refrigerated deli case. "What's up?"

"Oh, we found someone to work in the store, and we didn't put no ad in the paper." He turned and did a little cha-cha toward her in time with the music. "I'm so happy there's not gonna be a stranger in here." He grabbed her hands and swung her around. Despite his girth Dad was an incredible dancer. So was Mom.

Nikki ran through all the nearby relatives in her mind as she accidentally crushed her father's toes. "Is it Aunt Josie?" she asked.

"No."

"Uncle Nino?"

"Nope."

"Cousins John, Thomas, or Robby?"

"Eh, are you kidding me?" Dad asked with his palms together and shaking them at her, as if this was the most insane concept she'd ever come up with.

Nikki was really curious now. "Then *who*?"

Just as she asked, a flicker of movement caught in her peripheral vision. Nikki turned to find her mom in the kitchen doorway, resting her hands on the shoulders of a girl with a familiar short, dark 'do.

"Look who's going to be working with us this summer," Mom sang happily. "Your friend Hannah! Isn't that great?"

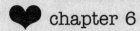 chapter 6

The next morning Nikki chose to forego breakfast at the family table in the deli and opted for a
yogurt in the back office and an emergency IM
gripe session with Blair.

YoNikkio: *Now I have to see her every
day. It's like some sick social experiment!*

Dare2Blair: *can't believe V & S did that 2
u! so cruel! don't they know u 2 aren't
bffs anymore?*

YoNikkio: *Negative. Didn't tell em. But
what's HER prob? SHE knows we're not
friends.*

Dare2Blair: *weird.*

YoNikkio: *Can't deal. Next subject pls.
How's the Muffmeister? How's ur tennis
swing? The towel hut? ;)*

Dare2Blair: *shut up! M is still in competition mode. now it's about a boy. a very cute one! meeting him in towel hut later. :-o (kidding!)*

YoNikkio: *Tell!!!!!!!*

Dare2Blair: *met him at Savannah's pool party. H-O-T! M saw us talking. so now she wants him. no big surprise there.*

YoNikkio: *Muffalicious has no chance. N-to-the-O, baby!*

Dare2Blair: *tell HER that. uh-oh. PGOS. gotta go!*

YoNikkio: *PGOS?*

Dare2Blair: *pilates guy over shoulder! got that big stupid ball w/him. TTYL! K?*

YoNikkio: *K. Bye!*

Nikki sighed, feeling a bit lonely and wishing that she had Blair to talk to full-time. She didn't even get to tell her about her date with Daniel. She resisted the urge to check out the RAG (Richfield Academy for Girls) blog on MySpace, knowing that it would only depress her, and logged off her mother's computer.

Well, I guess I've got to do this, she said silently, thinking about the awful day ahead, but really she was kind of hoping that Hannah would somehow get kidnapped by wild monkeys on her first day of work only to escape and find that Nikki's parents had canned Hannah for being late. Was that so wrong?

Nikki passed through the kitchen and into the deli and found the monkey whisperer herself sitting at the family table by the window — in *Nikki's* seat, no less.

Vince was laughing giddily. "I totally forgot how funny you are, Hannah. Where've you been hiding yourself lately?" A dorky grin appeared on his face.

No. He did not *just say that. Who says that?* Nikki wondered. To make things worse, it had been a full minute and a half and nobody had even noticed Nikki standing there. She cleared her throat. *"Ahem."*

"Oh, hi, Colie." Hannah glanced at her, then beamed at Nikki's family. And Nikki realized, to her nausea, that they were totally falling for Hannah's I'm-such-an-awesome-person con game. How could they be so gullible?

"It's *Nikki* now," she informed Hannah coolly.

"It is?" Dad asked as if this was the first time

he was hearing the news. "Since when do you change your name?"

"Since the Academy," Mom reminded him, "but we don't have to call her that."

What? For almost two years she'd been correcting them, practically *begging* to be called Nikki, and they didn't think the name applied to them? "Yes, you *do*!" she blurted out. "Everybody calls me Nikki except you people!"

"Eh, you better not be talking to your mother like that," Dad said in a stern voice. A deep crease emerged between his eyebrows as he furrowed them.

"Fine. Then I won't talk to *anybody*!" Nikki pivoted and stormed out of there. It took about fifteen steps before the regrets began. What felt like a red, hot rash crept up the back of her neck and around her ears. She didn't mean to throw a tantrum just then, but it was out there now and she couldn't take it back.

"Nicole Georgina Devita!" she heard her mom say, clearly pissed, but Nikki didn't turn back. How could she? It was too humiliating to face them all at once.

"Leave me alone!" she cried, knowing that it wasn't really what she wanted. Nikki waited in the kitchen for a moment to see if her mom or somebody would follow her back there. Then she could explain her case — that she didn't mean for it to come out that way. That she was upset over Hannah being hired. That they hadn't been friends since freshman year, and it hurt. It hurt to even look at her. It hurt so much that sometimes Nikki wanted to yell and cry and scream all at the same time. She wanted to explain all of it.

But nobody came.

Suck it up, Nikki, she thought as she pedaled her delivery route a little while later. What was that expression her father was always saying? *You make the bed, you lie in it.* Well, Nikki had chosen not to tell her parents about the trouble she'd been having with Hannah, so she shouldn't really be upset about them hiring her.

No, the best thing for Nikki to do was have as little human contact with the witch as possible and to keep her emotions in check and her mouth shut before her parents tried to get her a session with Dr. Phil.

Easier said than done.

Hannah was on sandwiches and getting the orders wrong left and right. By noon, Nikki had

had to make four extra runs. By closing time it had gone up to eight, and by the next afternoon, Nikki had had it.

She stomped into the kitchen with the latest offending sandwich, where Hannah was preparing chicken wrapped in prosciutto. "This is a panini. It's supposed to be hot and melty," Nikki explained, slapping it onto the counter. "Mrs. Arroyo wants another one. Try to get it right this time, okay?" Sure, it was snotty, but Hannah hadn't been exactly pleasant to work with, either.

"Maybe if you didn't take your sweet time delivering it," Hannah retorted, "it wouldn't be cold."

"I don't think so." Nikki tore open the wrapping and opened the raw sandwich. "Look, no grill marks on the bread and you can totally tell that this cheese was never melted," she said, proving her point.

Hannah shrugged. "So? What do you want me to do about it?"

"Look, just fix it, okay, Hannah?" Nikki said, pushing the panini toward the girl and thinking she might have seen a glimmer of amusement in her eyes. "Wait a sec, did you do this on *purpose*?" she asked, incredulous.

"If I did — and I'm not *saying* I did — you couldn't prove a thing." Hannah smiled. "Maybe you should fix that sandwich yourself. I'm busy," she said, sliding it back toward Nikki, then dumping a few cutlets into a bowl of flour.

Now Nikki finally got it. "You came here just to get on my nerves, didn't you? What's your problem?"

"I *came* here," Hannah replied, "because *you* got me fired from the jitney ticket booth and it was the only summer job left in a fifty-mile radius. Do you think I actually *want* to work in this hell-hole with you?"

Nikki positioned her hands on her hips. "First of all, I *told* you that was an accident. Second of all, I wouldn't have even *been* there if you and your little friends hadn't decided to prank me. And third of all, who do you think you are calling this place a *hellhole* when my parents were *nice* enough to offer you a job?" *Only I can call the Scallion a hellhole*, she thought. "So, be a good little worker and *make me a new sandwich*!" She tossed the sandwich back in Hannah's direction.

The panini landed in front of the girl with a slight bounce and a couple of wet tomato slices escaped, landing on Hannah's sandaled foot.

71

Hannah glanced at her foot, then glared at Nikki. *"No."* As she said this she chucked a handful of flour from her bowl onto Nikki's shirt.

"Hey!" Nikki immediately removed an egg from a nearby carton and flicked it at Hannah. The egg missed, and Hannah laughed. So Nikki snatched a raw chicken cutlet from the counter and slapped it onto Hannah's face.

"Arrrrrrrrr!" Hannah let out what sounded like a war cry and dumped the entire contents of her bowl over Nikki's head.

That was it. Soon eggs, flour, chicken, vegetables — anything Nikki could get her hands on — went flying at Hannah, and Hannah came back at her just the same. Nikki dodged a ripe tomato coming her way, then grabbed a handful of sliced prosciutto and whipped it hard at Hannah. Hannah ducked and the meat soared over her head toward the doorway just as Nikki's father entered the kitchen.

"What are you girls doing in here!" he said.

Nikki gasped as she watched, in what seemed like slow motion, as the prosciutto whirled through the air, landed on her father's forehead with a *slap*, and slid off. He caught it before it hit the floor, then, to Nikki's surprise, took a bite out of it.

That made Hannah and Nikki both laugh. Nikki stopped when she realized what the kitchen now looked like. Tomato splats on the walls and floor, macaroni dangling from the ceiling, every variety of vegetable and cheese strewn across the floor . . . "Oh, Dad . . ."

"I don't wanna know how this happened," Nikki's father said, gesturing around at the mess and clearly restraining his temper. "I wanna have this place clean in an hour." He looked from Nikki to Hannah, then back at Nikki. "And you'll both be working an extra shift to pay for this waste. You got me?"

"Yes, Dad," Nikki replied and went for the mop by the sink.

"We'll get it done," Hannah said, quickly peeling wilted lettuce leaves from the floor.

Nikki's father turned and exited and the two girls cleaned up in silence. Finally Hannah spoke up. "Look, I'm sorry, okay?" she said. "It was my mistake. I should have fixed the stupid sandwich."

Nikki nodded. "Thanks," she said. "I'm sorry, too. I could have been a little nicer about asking you." She paused, thinking. "Listen, I know we're not friends anymore, but let's at least try to be civil to each other," she offered. "Since we have to work together and all."

Hannah dumped a bunch of vegetables into the trash can next to Nikki and nodded. "Yeah, okay," she said. "Let's just get through the summer."

Nikki and Hannah spent the next hour sweeping and mopping and scrubbing down the kitchen in silence. So maybe they weren't friends, but at least they had come to a truce. For the summer, anyway.

chapter 7

Nikki was psyched for Saturday to finally arrive. Not only was it Hannah's day off and Nikki had had a blissful day at work but also Nikki was supposed to meet with Daniel.

According to Daniel they were slated to do something "a little different." The only problem was Nikki had no idea what they were doing or where they were supposed to meet. She'd tried calling him a couple of times on his cell yesterday but had only gotten his voice mail, and he hadn't called back yet.

How am I supposed to know what to wear if I don't know what we're doing? she wondered, staring into her closet. She crossed the room, snatched her cell phone off the dresser, and flipped it open. 3:22. Did he forget about their date? Should she call him again? No, that might seem a little too stalkerish. *But where was he?* she wondered.

She sat at her desk next to the dresser, turned on her computer, and logged on to the Internet. Maybe she'd send Blair an e-mail to pass the time. She clicked on the little mailbox icon and found that she had twelve messages. *Cool!* Had it really been Monday when she'd last logged on?

The first two were from a teen Web site she'd signed up for, inviting her to join some book club. *Delete. Delete.* The third was from a girl on MySpace asking her to rate the hotness of some guy. She clicked on the link to see a picture of a twenty-something blond guy with a six-pack stomach, wearing an electric blue bikini. Hmmm. Nine for the body, minus three for the poor choice in swimwear. She clicked on six, then delete. The rest of the e-mails were from anonymous spammers. *Deletedeletedeletedeletedeletedeletedelete deletedel* —

Wait! she thought, stopping her mouse. *This one isn't spam; it's from Daniel!* She clicked it open.

To: yonikkio@gmail.com
From: Danielthemaniel@yahoo.com

Re: Time, place, to do

Hey, Nikki!
Sorry been too busy to call. Hope ur up for a boat ride! Meet me at my aunt's house Saturday @ 4:00. Can't wait!
— Daniel

Nikki clicked on the printer icon and read the message again on the screen, a bit confused by it. What did it mean, "too busy to call"? What if she hadn't checked her e-mail? She would have never known what to do. Maybe he didn't care whether she showed up or not. But on the other hand he'd also written, "Can't wait," which in most circles meant that he was looking forward to seeing her. That is, if he was actually talking about *her* as opposed to the boat ride, which was also a possibility.

Nikki grabbed the e-mail from the printer and scanned it once more, realizing that he hadn't actually given her the address of his aunt's house. Now she *had* to call him.

Daniel picked up on the second ring. "Hello?"

"Hey, it's me," Nikki said. "I got your e-mail, but you forgot to tell me where you live."

"Oh. Sorry," Daniel said. "I thought you knew. It's on Winifred Lane."

Knew? How was she supposed to know if he'd never told her? "Okay, I think I know where that is. What's the number?"

"Uh, no number, Nikki. It's the only house." He said this as if Nikki was weird for even asking.

"Um, okay," Nikki said. "See you later." She flipped the phone shut. *Maybe it's best to* not *try to figure out boys*, she thought. At least it was easy to pick out a cute boaty outfit from her dresser. She slipped on a pair of white denim shorts, a blue-and-white striped halter, and a pair of navy flip-flops. She shoved her blue bikini in a bag just in case they decided to go for a dip. A quick fluff of the hair and she was out of the house in a flash.

Nikki groaned at first when she neared the jitney ticket booth and spotted Hannah hanging out by the counter talking to Margaret. Hannah saw Nikki, too, and greeted her with a slight lift of the chin. Nikki did the same in return, relieved that maybe the angry confrontations were finally over. Pressed for time, though, she rushed across town to the address Daniel had given her.

Winifred Lane was lined with a thicket of trees on either side and seemed more like a path in a forest preserve than a place where someone would have a home. She was beginning to wonder if maybe she was on the wrong street or something when the road spilled out onto the gated entrance of a grand estate.

A brass plaque was affixed to a high brick wall next to a double-sided iron gate with the letters *WB* embossed in gold. Underneath the letters was some sort of crest painted blue and white. Nikki inspected the plaque on the wall. It read BABCOCK MANOR.

No wonder Daniel thought I knew where he lived, Nikki thought, still gaping at the plaque. Daniel had mentioned his aunt Winnie a few times, but she hadn't made the connection until just now. *Whoa. Daniel's aunt is* the *Winnie Babcock*. Nikki didn't know the woman personally. In fact, she'd never even seen her. The only thing she did know was that Winnie Babcock was extremely wealthy and apparently, according to the rumors around town, quite eccentric.

"Nikki? Is that you?" Daniel's voice sounded from somewhere.

Nikki jumped, startled. She looked around and noticed a small intercom speaker on the gate and a TV camera at the top of the brick wall. The camera moved and focused and she gave it a little wave. "Hey, what's up, Daniel?"

"You have to use the intercom button," Daniel said through the speaker. "I can't hear you."

Nikki gave an exaggerated thumbs-up to the camera, then pressed the button underneath the speaker. "So are you going to let me in, or what?" she asked playfully.

"Oh, yeah. Heh, heh," Daniel replied.

A buzzer rang and Nikki watched as the iron gates slowly pushed open by themselves, revealing a gigantic limestone mansion, complete with imposing staircase and colorful English garden.

Nikki, feeling suddenly underdressed in her boaty outfit and flip-flops, wandered down a pebbled path that led through the garden overflowing with daisies, irises, roses, and thousands of other flowers that she had never seen before. Emerging from the garden, she found Daniel waiting for her by the foot of the staircase and was relieved to see him in a pair of old cutoffs and a T-shirt. *What did you expect him to be wearing, Nikki? A double-breasted navy blazer with khakis and a captain's hat?*

"I . . . I didn't —" Nikki began. How was she supposed to say that she didn't know his aunt was richer than God without sounding like a gold digger?

"I know," he finished for her. "I figured after you called that you didn't know I was a Babcock. And yes, my father *is* the big real estate tycoon," he said with a sigh, as if he'd answered that question ten thousand more times than he'd wanted to — ten thousand and one, actually.

Unfortunately, Nikki didn't know much about real estate and she had no idea to which tycoon he was referring. "So your dad's a realtor?" Nikki asked, trying to play it off. "Interesting."

Daniel tilted his head, amused. "You don't know who my dad is, do you?" he asked. "Preston Babcock? He's in all the financial dailies?" he asked.

Nikki shrugged. "Sorry. Don't read 'em."

"Me neither." Daniel grinned and took her hand, leading her up the staircase. "Let's go inside."

"So where are we going boating?" Nikki asked, looking around the place.

"You'll see," Daniel replied. "But first we have to have tea with Aunt Winnie. Is that okay?"

"Tea?" Nikki asked, feeling nervous again. "As in cucumber sandwiches and crumpets?"

81

"We use the term lightly at the Babcock abode," Daniel said. A butler dressed in a tux pulled open an enormous red door with a flourish and they entered into a foyer with a cathedral ceiling and a glittery chandelier overhead. A double staircase swept on either side of the house and met on the second-floor balcony. "My aunt should be down any minute," Daniel whispered, gazing up at the right staircase. "She likes to make an entrance."

Before Nikki knew it, dramatic music began to play from some unknown source. A second later Winnie Babcock appeared at the head of the stairs, wearing a black chiffon evening gown and a tiny diamond tiara in her salt-and-pepper-colored hair. She held Button in one hand as she floated downstairs, pausing every so often for dramatic effect.

Is she serious? Nikki wondered. The scene kind of reminded Nikki of an old black-and-white movie that she'd caught one insomniatic night on AMC. It was about some crazy old has-been movie star who was desperate to rekindle the fame of her youth. Unfortunately she just ended up looking demented as she prepared for her final close-up.

"Darrrrrrlings,"Winnie Babcock greeted them

when she reached the first floor. She held out a hand for Nikki to take and smiled warmly. *"Enchanté."*

Feeling totally out of her element, Nikki grasped the woman's hand and found herself doing a half-bow, half-curtsy kind of thing. "Um, pleased to meet you," she replied.

"Should we go into the study, Aunt Winnie?" Daniel asked.

"Yes, let's." Mrs. Babcock ushered them into a stately room bordered by bookcases containing tons of hardcover volumes. A beautiful round table with linens and china sat in front of a wall of floor-to-ceiling windows overlooking the back part of the grounds. Mrs. Babcock gestured to the table. *"Tea* is ready." She placed Button on the floor and the tiny dog scampered across the Oriental rug to sun herself by the windows.

Approaching the table, Nikki was surprised to find that the china was not filled with crustless cucumber sandwiches and the like, but Doritos, Cheese-ums, potato chips, Funions, caramel-covered popcorn, and the almighty Chex mix. As she sat, a butler tilted a teapot over her cup. Nikki took a sip. "Ooh. Dr Pepper," she said. "My favorite."

"Mine, too," Mrs. Babcock admitted. She grabbed a pair of silver tongs and used them to place a few Funions onto Nikki's plate. "And don't you just love these? They look like onions, they *taste* like onions, but they're definitely *not* onions."

Nikki took one and popped it into her mouth. "And so fun to eat!" she added, not really knowing what to think of all this.

After a stimulating conversation about favorite TV shows — apparently Mrs. Babcock was addicted to MTV's *The Real World*, but then again, who wasn't — it was time for the boat ride.

"Do you want to come with us, Mrs. Babcock?" Nikki asked, hoping that she'd join them. Mrs. Babcock might be a bit unconventional, but Nikki totally liked her.

"Oh, call me Winnie," Mrs. Babcock replied. "And no, I'm afraid I don't venture outside all that much these days. Have fun, kids."

"You were so cool with my aunt," Daniel said once they exited out a back door of the house. "But then I knew you would be. Thanks."

"I think she's interesting," Nikki said, really meaning it. "Has she always been so . . ."

"Weird?" Daniel finished. "I don't know. She's

filthy rich so she can act however she wants, and she doesn't care what people say about her. But I think she's just gotten bored over the years and does it to amuse herself."

"That's kind of cool," Nikki said.

Daniel nodded. "Well, she's never had to work, and she's not about to get a job at her age, and then there's the whole agoraphobia thing, so her charity work has kind of dwindled. She's definitely not crazy, though. She's the type of person who's got a lot of layers, you know?"

"She's complicated. Kind of like an onion," Nikki said.

"Or a *Funion*," Daniel added.

Nikki laughed, and she liked the way Daniel casually slipped his hand into hers as they made their way to a pier off a small channel. Nikki was expecting to see a canoe or a small speedboat or something, not the 45-foot sailboat that was in front of them. "You sure you can drive this thing?" she asked.

"Don't worry. I think there's a manual in the glove compartment," Daniel said, helping her onboard. Nikki gave him a wary look and he added, "I'm *kidding*. I practically grew up on a sailboat, so I know what I'm doing."

"Oh, yeah. I figured that," Nikki said casually, but was still a little relieved. She went belowdecks to change into her bikini and emerged back up top to find Daniel shirtless, and expertly maneuvering the sails of the boat.

"Okay, Nikki, when I give you the go, you undo that rope." He pointed to the one fastening them to the dock. A few seconds later he gave her the signal. "Go for it."

Nikki unlooped the rope and the boat slowly pushed away from the land and down the narrow channel. A few minutes later the channel widened a bit and the sails captured the breeze, zooming them along the outside edge of Richfield and finally depositing them into the harbor.

Nikki held on tightly as the boat bounced and cut through the waves. She spotted a familiar blue-and-white ship in the distance. "Look, the Bella Island jitney!" she called to Daniel.

Daniel nodded as he maneuvered through the harbor. Soon they were circling another familiar sight, Pelican Island. Daniel threw an anchor overboard and joined her on the bow of the boat with a couple of Cokes. As they leaned against a cushion, relaxing and rocking along with the choppy waves, Nikki gazed at her island. The fishing boats docked along the pier and the old colorful wood-frame homes seemed almost picturesque from this vantage point. A bit farther down the shore, workers were setting up cute game booths and a tall Ferris wheel for the upcoming festival next week.

"Pelican looks so different from out here," Nikki admitted to Daniel. "So quiet and beautiful. Not worn down and craggy like she is on the inside."

"I don't know about that. I think she's beautiful inside *and* out," Daniel said. He had a look in his eyes that Nikki didn't know quite how to decipher. He *was* talking about Pelican Island, wasn't he?

"I guess," Nikki said, turning back to the island. The sun was now casting an orangey-purple glow over the place she called home, and Nikki took a chance by resting her head on Daniel's shoulder as she watched the fishing boats return from a long day on the open waters. Daniel leaned his head on top of hers and the two sat there together for a while without talking. It was weird. Usually Nikki felt the need to fill up dead air with some kind of clever remark, but with Daniel it was different. With him, she felt comfortable enough to welcome the silence.

They watched as the orangish haze spread along the horizon behind Pelican Island. Nikki didn't want to spoil the moment, but with the sun setting she knew that she had to get back home. "My parents are expecting me for supper," she said reluctantly.

"Just a few more minutes," Daniel whispered, wrapping an arm around her shoulders and gazing at the colorful sky. "Okay?"

"All right." Nikki nuzzled closer to Daniel and sighed, enjoying the feel of him next to her, the beautiful vista, and the gentle swaying of the sea. "A few more minutes."

chapter 8

The next afternoon Nikki and her brothers helped their father close up shop at noon, while Mom went home to start on Sunday dinner. It was no secret that food was a big deal at the Devita house, but their Sunday ritual was especially festive. Mom usually cooked some kind of macaroni with meatballs and sausages, topped with a fresh sauce courtesy of the tomatoes and basil growing in the garden out back. If they were lucky, she'd bread and fry zucchini flowers, also from the garden, as a special treat.

They usually had some kind of company in the house that day, whether it was visiting relatives or neighbors stopping by for coffee and cake. So Nikki wasn't surprised when she heard the doorbell ring as she was clearing the dishes from the dining room table. When she opened the front door, however, her mouth dropped open. Hannah was standing there, holding a pastry box of some sort. Next to her were her parents, Agatha and Christian McVeigh, and her twelve-year-old brother, Billy.

Nikki's mom came clicking up behind her in denim short-shorts and her signature heels. "I'm so glad you made it. Hey, Vito, the McVeighs are here!" her mom called back toward the kitchen. "Colie, don't just stand there staring, let them in!"

"Oh. Right. Hi," Nikki greeted them and pushed open the screen door.

"Hey, Colie!" Mrs. McVeigh said.

"Long time no see, kid," Mr. McVeigh added as he and his wife entered the house.

"Where're Vince and Paul?" Billy asked as he stepped inside, too.

"Tossing a football out back," Nikki replied. "Why don't you go check it out?"

Hannah handed Nikki the pastries and slid by with no eye contact.

Could we get any more uncomfortable? Nikki wondered as she followed them all into the formal living room — the one Nikki and her brothers weren't allowed to enter unless guests were around.

"Make yourselves at home," Nikki's mom told the McVeighs, gesturing to the newish-looking green furniture set that was really twenty years old. "I'm going to put the coffee on."

"I'll help," Nikki offered. But really she just wanted to get out of the same room as Hannah. Once she was in the kitchen she turned to her mom. "Why did you invite them over here?" she whispered.

Stella Devita rolled her eyes. "Is this about that little argument you and Hannah had at the Scallion? I thought you two would be over that by now."

"No, it's . . . it's . . ." Nikki wanted to say that it was more than the kitchen incident, that she and Hannah were only being civil to each other so that they'd make it through the summer without somebody bursting a blood vessel. But did she really want to open that can of worms when there was nothing Mom, or anybody, could do about it? "Never mind," she said. "Forget it."

"Okay, then bring this out to the McVeighs." Her mom took the box from her, opened it, and placed the assorted pastries on a serving plate.

Nikki did as she was told, placing the platter on the marble coffee table in front of Mr. and Mrs. McVeigh. Hannah was slouched in an armchair by the window, so Nikki took the one at the opposite end of the room.

Nikki felt Hannah's eyes bore into her as she sat, and she willed herself not to look back. "So . . ." Nikki began, but she was drawing a blank on the engaging small talk and feeling very awkward. Good thing Rocky trotted into the room and over to Nikki. "Hey, boy!" she said, and busied herself by rubbing his belly, then scratching behind his ears, hoping she'd seem too occupied to make conversation.

Nikki was relieved not only when her parents arrived with the coffee but when she received a text message.

Saved by the Blair, she thought cheesily, and pulled her phone out from her jeans pocket to read the screen.

Muffy strikes again!

the saga continues . . .

r u ready 4 . . .

episode 2?

Nikki smiled and began to text back a response.

Go 4 it!

"Nikki, it's not nice to text in front of company," her mother scolded her.

"Oh, sorry. You're right, Mom. It's, like, so rude of me," Nikki said as she began standing. "Um, but I kind of have to take this. It's important," she added, backing out of the room. "Be right back. Okay?" She exited without waiting for an answer and headed up the stairs to her bedroom — with no intention of returning. It was just too weird and tense hanging out with the McVeighs.

She flopped onto her bed to read Blair's next message.

'member pool party guy?

M had hots for him . . .

but crash 'n' burned!!!!

PPG likes me and M can't STAND it!

what up w/ur hottie?

Nikki quickly ran her thumbs over the keys on her phone:

I ❤ Mr. Hottie!

Think maybe he ❤ me too!

Blair wrote back:

Good kisser?

Nikki didn't know about that so she typed in:

Dates: 3

Kisses: 0

Nikki hesitated before pressing SEND. Did it seem lame to have had three dates and zero kisses? She wasn't about to throw herself at Daniel, but it wasn't as if she'd been playing hard to get, either. So how come he hadn't even *tried* to make out with her — not even yesterday on their romantic sunset cruise? What was the deal?

Cut it out, Nikki told herself. *Stressing will only give you zits. Besides, he wouldn't keep asking you out if he didn't like you ... right?*

Just as she'd decided to listen to her inner dating guru, someone knocked on the door. *Probably Mom*, she thought. "Just a minute!" she called, then typed in:

Gotta go. Later!

Then she pressed SEND and hopped off her bed to open her door. "Oh. It's you," she said, observing Hannah standing in the hallway.

"Yeah. The parents told me to get lost. They've got to talk about some adult stuff. I don't know."

"Why don't you hang with the guys outside, then?" Nikki suggested. "They're in the backyard with your brother."

"Not anymore," Hannah said. "I don't know where they are. So I guess we're stuck with each other." With this she pushed past Nikki into the room.

No, we're not. You could go read a magazine in some dark corner somewhere. Nikki kept that thought to herself, though, not wanting to start an argument.

"You got a new bedspread," Hannah commented, nodding as if she approved. Then she moved to the bookcase next to Nikki's desk. "I can't believe you still have this." She picked up a pink glitter-gelled plastic picture frame. "I made this for you in, like, fourth grade or something." Hannah held on to it a little longer, and Nikki could tell that she was inspecting the photo inside the frame.

It used to hold a close-up of Hannah and Nikki hugging and smiling at the camera. They had taken the picture during the summer after seventh grade, the first time they were allowed to go to the local beach on their own. Now the frame held a photo of Nikki and Blair in English class mugging for the camera in matching cabbie hats and doing their "angry model" poses.

Nikki wondered what Hannah was thinking. Was she upset about the whole I-hate-your-guts thing, too? Maybe coming up to Nikki's room was Hannah's way of reaching out?

"I want to show you something," Nikki said. She took the frame from Hannah's hands, then slid out the old picture of Nikki and Hannah, which was hiding underneath the new one of Nikki and Blair. "See? I didn't get rid of it."

Hannah turned away, shrugging casually. "So? Do you think I care?"

Nikki frowned. "You know, I don't get you. I'm trying to be nice here, Hannah. What more do you want from me?"

Hannah spun around. "I don't want anything

from you, Colie. Oh, sorry, I mean *Nicole* or whatever you're calling yourself these days."

"Nikki."

"Whatever, *Nikki*." Hannah spat out her name as if it tasted bad. "The only reason I'm here is because my parents made me come. Don't think I want to be friends with you because I *don't*. Not with someone like you."

What's that supposed to mean? Someone like me? The words stung, but Nikki didn't want Hannah to know that. "Well, the only reason *I'm* here is because I *live* here. And this is *my* room, and if you think I'm so awful, why don't you just get out?"

"Fine." Hannah made a swift turn for the door. "I'm out!"

"Fine!" Nikki repeated. "And I don't want to be friends with you, either!" Okay, so maybe she did. A little. She flopped face-first onto her bed, knowing that their truce was over, though not fully understanding how it had happened. She hugged her pillow and let out a deep sigh.

A few seconds later she felt a hand gently touch her arm. It was Hannah. "Hey, I didn't mean to make you cry," she said. "Really."

Could it be? Was Hannah actually being nice?

Nikki turned to face her. "It's okay. I'm not crying."

"Oh. When I saw your face in the pillow . . ." Hannah almost seemed embarrassed. "Well, I'd better go."

"Wait," Nikki said, stopping her. She saw an in — probably her one and only opportunity to make peace — and she was going for it. "I . . . I just have to know something, Hannah," she began slowly. "Why do you . . . *hate* me so much?" There. It was out, and Hannah could either answer the question or leave. It was up to her.

Hannah folded her arms across her chest. "Why do you hate *me* so much?"

"I don't hate you," Nikki replied. She didn't. Not deep inside.

"Then why are you so mean to me?" Hannah replied.

"Me? Mean to *you*?" Nikki sat up in her bed. "Are you kidding? You're the one who's mean to *me*!"

"Only because you started it," Hannah admitted. "And to make things worse you start hanging out with those Richfield Academy snots. I mean, give me a break. You're best friends with the queen brat!"

98

Nikki leaned against her headboard. "First of all, how did *I* start it when *you* were the one who'd stopped returning my calls?" she said. "It totally *killed* me."

Hannah was about to say something but seemed to change her mind. "It did?" she asked.

"I didn't know what was going on," Nikki admitted. "And I wanted to talk to you about it, but you wouldn't call me back. And then there's Blair. She's *so* not a snob. It was tough making friends at the Academy. They all knew one another since kindergarten and I was the pathetic new girl on scholarship. And if it weren't for Blair I'd probably still be eating lunch alone. Besides, did you really expect me to go friendless over there?"

Hannah hesitated. "No, but I *did* expect you to stay the same. Instead you turned into this totally preppy Richfield snob who thinks she's the greatest thing since the iPod. As if, now that you're an Academy girl, you're too good for Pelican Island or something."

Nikki surveyed the red-and-white striped Abercrombie polo shirt and knee-length shorts she was wearing. "Okay, so maybe you have a point about the preppiness, and maybe I *have* changed a little — maybe you have, too — but Hannah, I don't think I'm better than anybody. I swear!"

Hannah played with a loose thread sticking out of the seam of her jeans. "That's not what Margaret and Stephanie told me you told *them*."

"And you *believed* those two?" Nikki asked. "Why?"

Hannah shrugged and glanced away for a minute. When she turned back she stared directly into Nikki's eyes. "You know I had nothing to do with their prank phone call, right?" she asked, turning back timidly.

She seems so sincere, Nikki thought, this time believing her. "Yeah," she said. "I know."

Hannah sat on the edge of Nikki's bed and sighed. "Okay, so maybe I was a *tiny* bit jealous and felt a *little* left out when you started at the Academy," she said. "God, I can't believe I just told you that."

Nikki leaned forward and touched her old friend's arm. "Believe me, Hannah, I never wanted to leave you out. I still don't."

"So, maybe we can start over?" Hannah asked. "Hang out a little? Be friends again?"

Nikki nodded. "Okay," she said, not certain if

their friendship would ever be the way it was but definitely willing to give it a try.

A soft knock sounded on the bedroom door before it opened and Nikki's mother entered. "I thought you girls might need this," she said, offering them a gigantic bowl of buttery popcorn.

The twinkle in her mom's eyes along with her devilish grin made Nikki suspect that Mom had orchestrated this whole reunion. *Very sneaky, Mom,* she thought, taking the bowl off her hands, glad to know that she had such a devious mother.

chapter 9

On Friday night Daniel and Nikki strolled hand in hand underneath a sky of colorful glowing lanterns during the second night of the Bait 'n' Tackle Festival on Pelican Island. The opening had been last night, complete with music and fireworks, but Daniel couldn't make it. That was okay. He and Nikki were having an awesome time. They'd already tried the bumper cars, done the Rock 'n' Roll ride, and rode the Ferris wheel.

"How about the fish?" Daniel asked, pausing in front of a booth that was holding a slippery tuna-catching contest. "What do you think?"

"Why not? I'll back you up," Nikki said. "But just to let you know, my brother Vince did that last year and he reeked for a whole week . . . I mean, more than he usually does."

Daniel held up his hands. "Maybe I'll pass on the tuna. Thanks."

Nikki enjoyed a hefty bite from her powdered funnel cake, then spotted something a little more her speed. "Hey, look. They're having a watermelon-eating contest over there!"

"Would you believe I won one of those things when I was eight?" Daniel said, patting his wash-board abs. "Aunt Winnie says I'm an excellent eater."

"Really?" Nikki asked. "Well, then you *have* to do it! Come on, I'll do it, too, okay?"

"I'm down," Daniel said. "Let's go."

They joined the table of competitors, grabbing seats behind two enormous slices of watermelon just as the next contest was about to begin. Mr. Farricker, the man running the booth, went over the only rule: no hands.

Daniel pointed to one of the gigantic blue elephants sitting on a high shelf, then pointed to Nikki, indicating that he was going to win it for her. Nikki grinned and gestured to a huge stuffed eggplant on the shelf below, then nodded at Daniel.

A second later a whistle was blown and the contestants shoved their faces into their water-melons. Nikki had taken maybe four bites when the whistle was blown again. "We have a winner!" Mr. Farricker called out.

"That's impossible!" Nikki cried. She and Daniel exchanged a glance, amazed, as a skinny kid about sixteen picked out a blue dragon with shiny gold lamé wings and handed it to the girl next to him.

Next Nikki and Daniel went to the basketball toss, the sharpshooter, then the game where you shoot the water into a clown's mouth until the balloon attached to its head bursts. After a second whirl on a rickety Ferris wheel they followed the sound of music down to the end of the game aisle, stopping in front of a large tent. A kind of swingy, bluesy tune that Daniel seemed really into was blaring from inside.

He bobbed his head to the beat. "Hey, want to check it out?" he asked.

"Sure," Nikki said, following him through the entranceway.

The place was packed with people of all ages, shapes, and sizes totally wigging out to the music. On the stage was a tall skinny guy in an oversize suit and a fedora singing an old-fashioned swing song from the 1940s. To his left was a short guy in a matching suit, wagging his head and playing a bass that was as tall as he was. Another guy in a suit strummed a catchy tune on his guitar and behind them was a girl, also in a large suit, jamming on the drums.

"Man, I wish I knew how to dance," he said, staring at the people on the dance floor. "It looks like fun." Couples were performing choreographed steps and spinning around like crazy. One guy swung his partner to the left, then the right, then over his head before setting her down on her feet. She squealed in delight, then did a flirty little shimmy and continued dancing.

"I can show you if you want," Nikki offered.

"You know how?" Daniel seemed doubtful.

"What? You don't believe me?" Nikki pretended to be offended. "I may not be as good as my parents but, thanks to them, I do know how to swing dance. Come on. It's easy. Just follow me," she said, leading him onto the floor. She turned to face him and took his hands. "This is a basic rock step. One-two-three, one-two-three, back-front . . . one-two-three, one-two-three, back-front . . ."

Daniel tried to follow the steps she was showing him. "One-two-three. One-two —"

"Ow!" Nikki cried after he'd crushed her foot.

"Sorry!" Daniel said. "I'm not so good at this." He listened to the band and bopped to the beat a bit, trying to loosen up. "Okay, I'm ready," he said. "One-two —"

"Ah!" Nikki cried out when he accidentally kicked her ankle.

They tried a little longer, but by the time the third song had ended Daniel was ready to stop. Nikki followed him to an empty table just off the dance floor. But the beat of the music was so infectious that Nikki didn't want to sit down. She bounced and tapped her foot to the beat.

"Go ahead," Daniel said, motioning back to the dance floor. "I'll watch you. I don't mind. Really."

"Just one dance," she said, then smiled at an older gentleman who was standing along the edge of the dance floor nearby. He held out a hand and she took it, then followed him to the center of the dancers.

They started out with a simple rock step but soon she and the man were performing intricate dance steps and swinging around each other with their hands in the air. The man weaved her in and out of spins as they bounced and jived to the swingy tune. Finally, they ended the dance with a low dip, inches from the floor.

Wow. This guy is almost as good as my dad, Nikki thought, smiling and thanking him for the awesome dance and, for the first time, noticing that several of the other couples had stopped to watch them perform.

Nikki and the man parted ways as the next song began. She clapped and bopped her head in time with the music, scanning the faces of the crowd as she crossed over to where Daniel was sitting. She stopped short when she came across two familiar ones. "Mom and Dad," she breathed.

It's not as if they didn't know she'd be at the festival, but they didn't know that she'd be at the festival with a boy. Maybe she should have kept a lower profile. Dad was sure to create a scene. *Why haven't you introduced us? You know the rules, we have to meet him first . . .* yadda, yadda, yadda. She wanted them to find out about Daniel at some point, just not like this.

At that same moment, Mom waved from across the room in Nikki's direction.

Uh-oh. She spotted me, Nikki thought, pretending not to see her and heading for the back door of the tent. She passed by Daniel's table and discreetly motioned for him to follow her outside.

He did.

"What's up?" he asked, stepping through the doorway, which unfolded onto a spread of sandy beach.

"It was getting hot in there." Nikki slipped off her shoes and took his hand, leading him toward the water and away from the tent.

"Hey, you were awesome out there," he said. "My mom tried to get me to take ballroom dancing lessons when I was a kid but unfortunately I was born with two left feet."

Nikki made a special effort to inspect them. "They seem okay to me," she said, not caring if it was corny. "Seriously, though, it's hard to learn when everybody is rocking out around you. I could teach you now, if you want."

"I'll try, but I'm not promising results," Daniel said, lacing his fingers through hers.

"Basic rock step?" Nikki asked as they tried the dance.

"So far, so good," Daniel said. Then he attempted to spin her, but they ended up in a tangled mess.

"You're right. It's hopeless," she said, laughing after several failed attempts.

"Maybe I just need a different kind of dance," Daniel suggested, still holding her. He paused, seeming to listen to the music in the distance. The band was now playing an old crooning ballad from the 1950s. "Here," he said, almost shy now, taking a step closer and placing his hands lightly on her waist.

Instinctively, Nikki wrapped her arms around his neck. No need for special steps—they barely lifted their feet off the sand as their bodies swayed to the music.

Nikki felt a delightful shiver as Daniel pulled her closer and lowered his head so that their cheeks were barely touching. "See? This dance is nice, too," he murmured softly.

"Mmm-hmm," Nikki said, breathing in the light, clean scent of his cologne. The moonlight cast a romantic shimmer across the gentle sea. If ever there were a moment perfect for a first kiss, this would be it. *Kiss me, Daniel,* she said silently. *I want you to kiss me....*

Daniel stopped dancing and loosened their embrace so that he could see her. His piercing blue eyes gazed into hers. He was serious now. No more banter as he leaned toward her, his lips coming closer.

Nikki closed her eyes and tilted her head to the right, ready to accept his kiss . . . and to return it. *He's going to do it*, she thought. *He's really going to . . .*

"Nicole Georgina Devita!" Her mother's voice pierced through the moment like a dagger.

Daniel sprang away in an instant. Nikki gazed over his shoulder and spotted the familiar silhouettes of her parents. *No!* she silently cried. *No, no, no! They couldn't have waited two more seconds?!*

Apparently not, since they were now marching away from the tent and toward the water.

"Are those your parents?" Daniel asked. She couldn't tell if that was fear she heard in his voice or just curiosity.

"Yeah. Wait here, okay?" Nikki replied.

Daniel stayed put as Nikki jogged to meet her parents.

"Eh, who is that boy?" Dad asked, staring past her at Daniel, who was looking pretty uncomfortable. "You got a boyfriend and you don't tell us?"

"You know the rules," Mom said. "You're not allowed to date a boy until we meet him."

"I know, I know," Nikki agreed. "I was going to introduce you. . . ."

"When?" Dad asked, folding his arms across his burly chest.

Nikki knew that she should have taken care of this earlier. Now there was nothing else she could do. "How about during Sunday dinner?" she suggested.

chapter 10

"Do *not* embarrass me," Nikki told Vince and Paul Sunday afternoon as she placed dishes on the dining room table for dinner.

"Oh, we are *so* going to embarrass you," Vince said. He removed six glasses from the china cabinet and set them on the table. "We wouldn't be doing our brotherly duty if we didn't. Right, Paul?" he called into the living room.

"Yup." Paul was busy picking through the box of assorted Italian chocolates on the coffee table that Mom had brought from the store for the occasion.

"Okay," Nikki said casually. "Just remember this, Vince. I know all the humiliating details of your life. So when you finally get the nerve to ask out a girl, I'll be fully loaded."

Vince blushed. "Who says I'm going to ask out anyone? I mean, I don't even know why you would think that." He chuckled a little, then turned to Nikki.

Paul leaned on the edge of the opening that separated the living room and the dining room. "Smooth, Vince. Nikki has no idea that you like someone now." He turned back and flopped into an armchair, hanging a leg over the side.

"Paul!" Vince cried.

"Wait a sec." Nikki followed him into the living room. "What did you just say?"

Paul shrugged. "What? About Vince liking someone?" he asked.

"Oh, who cares if Vince likes someone?" Nikki said. "I mean, *before* that. You called me *Nikki*. Thanks!"

"Well, after you made such a big deal about it the other day, how could I not?" Paul said, just as the doorbell rang.

"Oh my God, he's here!" Nikki gulped, raced into the hallway, and checked herself in the mirror above the console. Then she answered the door. Daniel looked so cute standing there in his baggy jeans and polo shirt and holding a bouquet of daisies. Nikki considered casually kissing him hello, but chickened out. Instead she pushed open the screen door and said, "Hey."

"Hey," Daniel replied, stepping inside. "What's up?"

Nikki glanced at the daisies he was holding at his side. *He brought me flowers*, she thought. *Is he sweet or what?*

"Oh. For your mom." He held them out. "For inviting me. Do you think that's sucking up too much?" he asked.

Actually, if Nikki wanted to be technical about it, *she* had invited him, not her mom. "No. No way. She'll love it." Nikki tried not to let her disappointment sound in her voice. "Let's go show them to her." She led him inside the house. "Mom! Daniel's here!"

Mom emerged from the kitchen wearing a boxy housecoat snapped closed from top to bottom and a pair of black pumps. "The lasagna's just about ready," she said, wiping her hands on a dish towel and smiling at Daniel.

But Nikki was still staring at her mom's clothes. Was it a weird attempt at modesty? Somehow it didn't seem right on her mother. "Hey, Mom. What's the deal with the dowdy outfit? You feeling okay?"

Mrs. Devita glanced down at the multicolored material. "Oh, this? I didn't want to get dirty cooking." She popped the snaps open in a flash, exposing her black leather skirt and fuzzy purple tank. "*Shazam!*"

Surprised, Nikki couldn't help but laugh at her mom, who had clearly planned that. She glanced at Daniel, who was also laughing.

"These are for you, Mrs. Devita," he said, handing her the bouquet.

"Oh, how nice!" she said. "Let me put these in some water. You kids go sit down. I'll be out in a minute with your father, Colie — I mean, Nikki."

"Thanks, Mom," Nikki said. She appreciated the effort.

"Your mom's cool," he said, taking a place at the table. "I like her already."

"I think she likes you, too," Nikki whispered. *One down, three to go*, she thought.

Then Paul and Vince came in and took seats across from Nikki and Daniel. "So, this is Bucky," Paul said.

Vince snickered, and Nikki instantly regretted telling him that Daniel was, indeed, the "Buck-o" from the phone a couple of weeks ago.

"'Bucky'?" Daniel repeated, confused.

"Never mind," Vince said. "Must be some other guy." He and Paul were obviously preparing to torture her through the entire dinner.

Thank goodness Mom and Dad entered the room with plates of hot and cold antipasti, an

115

extremely large pan of lasagna, a dish of meat-balls, a fresh salad, and some semolina bread. Mom placed the lasagna on the buffet to cool while they ate the antipasti.

"So," Dad said, eyeing Daniel and chewing on a piece of honeydew melon wrapped in prosciutto. "You like my daughter. How did you meet?"

Uh-oh. Nikki gulped. Knowing it would have upset her father, she'd kind of neglected to mention the major wipeout on the brand-new Scallion-cycle. She braced herself for the story.

"Well, Nikki almost ran me over one day with her bike," Daniel began, "and then she slipped and fell off it and —"

"I *knew* it!" Vince suddenly jumped out of his seat and did a cocky double index-fingered point at Paul. "You owe me my five bucks back plus five of your own, bro!" he exclaimed with glee.

"Wait. You guys bet on if I'd fall off the delivery bike?" Nikki asked, her cheeks burning as the rest of the table cracked up.

"On your first day," Vince added, still laughing. "The odds were in my favor."

Paul reached into his pocket, slapped a ten-spot on the table, and shook his head. "I should have known, man. I should have known."

The remainder of dinner was filled with joking, a bit more teasing, and a lot of easy conversation. Daniel seemed fascinated by her dad's travels from small-town Sicily to small-town New England. And Vince and Paul were totally looking forward to a ride on the Babcock sailboat.

"Dan, you're okay," Vince said, finishing his last bite of lasagna. He leaned back in his chair and rubbed his stomach. "Ugh, I think I ate too much."

"I'll take that as a compliment," Mom said, wiping her mouth.

"Hey, Danny. You play football?" Paul asked. "We could get a game of touch going in the backyard. Burn off some of those meatballs."

Nikki kicked Paul underneath the table. She was looking forward to a little alone time with Daniel.

"Ow!" Vince cried. "What was that for?"

Oops! Missed, she thought. "Sorry."

"Sure. Why not?" Daniel said, then turned to Nikki. "Want to play, too? Me and you against these guys?"

How could Nikki say no to that? "We'll wipe the floor with them," she said.

* * *

"Show them how to do it, Nikki!" Mom cheered from the back porch while Dad sipped a tiny cup of espresso.

"Hut one, hut two, hike, hike!" Nikki shouted. The score was fourteen to seven, and Nikki and Daniel had one more chance to make a touchdown and tie the game. Otherwise the twins would win.

Vince was standing in front of her with his hands up, ready to block her pass. "One Mississippi, two Mississippi . . ." If he reached ten before she threw it, he'd tackle her.

Daniel faked left and right behind her. Then he rushed forward toward the goal line ready to make the play. Paul scrimmaged to catch up to Daniel as Nikki spiraled the football right into Daniel's hands.

"Go! Go! Go!" Nikki screamed as Daniel ran to make the touchdown. Vince turned and gave chase along with Paul but they were too far behind. It looked as if Daniel was going to make it!

Until he tripped over the long chain, which dangled out of his pocket, then tumbled to the ground. "Oof!"

"Oh, yeahhhhhh!" Paul ceremoniously tapped Daniel's back with his hands, and the game was over. Then Paul and Vince did their little ducklike happy dance and slapped each other five.

"You okay, Daniel?" Nikki asked, jogging over to him.

Daniel nodded. "Just a little embarrassed," he admitted, stuffing the chain that was attached to his wallet into his back pocket.

"Hey, Danny boy!" Vince yelled. "You might want to rethink the antipickpocket device next time." He doubled over, cracking up.

"Maybe you shouldn't be so smug, my friend," Daniel said teasingly. "Next time I might not let you win!"

"You'd better come up now if you don't want your dad to eat all the dessert!" Mom called from the porch, followed by an "Eh, Stella! Come on. It's Sunday!" from Dad.

Nikki, Daniel, and her brothers climbed the three steps to the deck and joined their parents for some tartuffo and coffee. They talked about everything from the state of the nation to how disgusting it is when people clip their fingernails in public. And Nikki actually found herself enjoying the conversation . . . and the company. *We should do this more often*, she thought, gazing at her family. *It's kind of fun.*

Before long it was time for Daniel to go home. "You're so lucky," he said as they strolled through the side yard to the front. "You have such an awesome family."

Nikki couldn't dispute that. Okay, it was true that her parents were a little overprotective and her brothers superannoying at times, but there was no doubt that they'd always be there for her. And she'd be there for them, too. "I think I'll keep them," she said.

Daniel turned to her when they reached the white picket fence in the front yard. "You know, I'm really glad I met you, Nikki."

"You are?" Nikki asked, excited. Was this the part where he tells her how beautiful she is and professes his undying love?

Daniel nodded. "Yeah. I thought I was going to be stuck spending the entire summer alone with Aunt Winnie and Button. But then I started hanging out with you, and you invited me here, and I met your family, and . . . I, um, I just wanted to say . . ."

"*Yes?*" Nikki asked, taking a step closer. Who knew? He just might want to kiss her!

"Well . . . thanks for being such a good friend." Daniel balled his left hand into a fist and gave her a little mock punch on the side of her arm — *again*. "I really appreciate it." With that he pushed open the front gate, stepped onto the sidewalk, and waved good-bye.

A good friend? Nikki thought, touching the spot where Daniel had just hit her and watching him disappear around the corner. *Is that all I am to him? A friend?*

chapter 11

"He said he *appreciates* your *friendship*?" Hannah asked the next morning in the back office of the Italian Scallion. "What's that supposed to mean?"

"Don't ask me. I don't get it, either," Nikki replied. "I mean, one minute he's all, let's enjoy my sailboat at sunset or slow dance underneath the moonlight, and the next he's giving me friendly punches in the arm like I'm his sister or something."

"Maybe you're not giving him the *signal*, you know?" Hannah suggested hopefully. She rustled inside her blue backpack that was on the floor beside Mom's desk and pulled out the latest issue of *Cosmo*. "I think there's an article in here that tells you how to do it right."

Nikki rolled her eyes. "I don't think there's a right way or wrong way to let a boy know you want him to kiss you."

"*Excuse* me?" Hannah gave Nikki a look that

said, *Mind getting real for a sec?* "Let's face it," she said. "You're not exactly getting any, so why don't you humor me, all right?"

"Okay, okay." Nikki sighed and sat in her mom's rolling desk chair. "Go."

"Cool." Hannah flipped through the magazine until she came to a page with the headline FIVE POINTERS TO MAKE HIM PUCKER.

"Are you kidding me?" Nikki asked, reading the title.

"*Go* with it," Hannah said with feeling. "Okay. Number one: Body contact is key, such as touching his arm or face."

"*Only* his arm or face?" Nikki asked with a devilish grin.

"Be nice," Hannah replied. "Number two: Pout your lips every time he looks your way. They will seem irresistibly plump and very kissable. Three: Wear flavored lip gloss and casually comment on how delicious it tastes."

"Oh, *that's* subtle," Nikki said with a laugh.

Hannah glared at Nikki for a second, then went back to the tips. "Say *kiss me* by gazing into his eyes, then at his lips, then into his eyes again. Don't forget to lick *your* lips. He'll be sure to get the message."

"Ew! Ditto on the subtle-o," Nikki commented.

Hannah laughed before she read the last pointer aloud. "Oh, you're going to *love* this one. It's sort of the combo platter of pucker pointers. You ready?" she asked.

Nikki wasn't sure, but she nodded, anyway. "Read it."

"Five: If all else fails, pout your lips, gaze at his mouth, then into his eyes seductively while licking your lips and commenting on how delicious your lip gloss tastes!"

Hannah and Nikki burst out laughing.

"That's ridiculous!" Nikki cried. "Who reads this garbage?" she asked, still giggling.

Hannah held up the magazine. "Guilty. It's a subscription." Then she pouted. "How do I look? Think a boy will want to kiss me?"

"I don't know. What flavor is your lip gloss?" Nikki said, and they laughed again. *This is nice*, she thought, realizing at that very moment just how much she missed hanging out with her old pal. "So, what do you think I should do about my situation, Hannah? How am I supposed to find out if he likes me as more than a friend?"

Hannah sat on the edge of the desk, thinking. She seemed about to say something but hesitated.

"What?" Nikki asked. "You were going to say something."

Hannah shrugged. "Maybe . . ." She paused as if she were trying to figure out how to put it. "Maybe he likes you as more than a friend but . . . this is so out there I don't even know if I should say it."

"You *have* to tell me now," Nikki said. "You can't just leave me hanging like this. Say it fast; it'll be easier."

"Well, maybe he's got another girlfriend," Hannah said sheepishly. "And he *can't* kiss *you* because then he'd be cheating on *her*. This way he can fool himself into thinking that you guys are only friends — just as long as he doesn't kiss you, that is, even though he probably *wants* to."

Nikki could tell that Hannah was speaking from the heart, but that didn't mean she was right. "No way," Nikki said, shaking her head. "Daniel's so awesome. Such a good guy. And sweet. And he would never do something like that. . . ." She trailed off, considering Hannah's theory again. It *did* explain the mixed messages she was getting from him. "Would he?" she added.

"Maybe not," Hannah said. "Let's think. Is he ever, like, mysteriously unavailable at times? As if he disappeared from the planet or something?"

Nikki thought about it. There *were* a few times when she couldn't get in touch with him. Like the time before she went to the Babcock estate. Instead of calling her back he'd sent an e-mail. And then again when she'd tried to set up their date at the festival, she couldn't get in touch with him until late in the week, too. Even then he couldn't go on opening night and he never *did* say why. Nikki hadn't thought anything of it at the time, but now it was beginning to bug her. Where was he hiding out? What was the big secret?

"Now that I think about it, he doesn't seem to be around on Tuesdays, Wednesdays, and Thursdays." She gazed at Hannah with her mouth open. "You don't think . . ."

"Let's not think anything," Hannah said, touching her shoulder. "Not until we know what's up."

"But I can't just call him and ask him," Nikki

told her. "What if we're totally wrong? I'll be humiliated — and he might end up hating me."

"True . . ." Hannah said, thoughtful. "Hey, do you know where he lives?" she asked.

Nikki nodded. "Uh-huh."

"Well, you're off tomorrow and Tuesday's a slow day, so I can call in sick. . . ."

"And?" Nikki prompted her.

"And we can just happen to be hanging out over there tomorrow morning and see where Daniel goes," she said.

"Like two psycho stalkers?" Nikki asked, doubtful. "I don't think so."

"*Stalker* makes it sound so, oh, I don't know . . . *dirty*," Hannah replied. "I was thinking more along the lines of *detective*. You *do* want to find out what the deal is, right?"

That was the thing. She did. But did she want to do it *this* way?

"I can't believe I actually let you talk me into this," Nikki told Hannah early the next morning as they walked their bikes through the brush that bordered Winifred Lane. A twig from a low-hanging tree snapped her cheek. "Ow!"

"Shh!" Hannah covered Nikki's mouth with one hand and pointed to the Babcock estate up ahead with the other. "I think someone's coming out," she whispered. "Look!"

Sure enough, the iron gates were opening. A second later a boy zoomed out of the gate and past them on a red ten-speed. Daniel. He was wearing his usual uniform of enormous shorts and an oversize tee and had an army pack strapped to his back. Nikki wondered where he was going in such a rush.

"What are we waiting for?" Hannah said. "He'll get away!"

The girls pushed their bikes onto the road and pedaled fast to catch up enough to see where Daniel was going, still remaining a safe distance behind. Nikki prayed that he wouldn't look back and spot them following him.

He didn't. Instead he made a sharp left at the corner of Winifred and Main and stopped off at a bakery. Nikki was pretending to look at postcards on a rack outside a drugstore a few doors down when Daniel emerged with six croissants and a bottle of strawberry Yoo-hoo. She watched him down all six croissants in a matter of seconds. "Uh-oh. Looks like he's got a serious problem with French pastries," Nikki said as she watched him swallow his last bite, then proceed to chug the Yoo-hoo. She turned to Hannah. "Good thing I found out about this early. Thanks, Nancy Drew."

"Hey, I thought we should see what he's up to. I never said it'd be *interesting*," Hannah replied.

Daniel tossed his garbage into a trash bin, mounted his bike, and took off again.

"Check it out," Hannah said. "He's leaving." She hopped on her bike and pedaled away.

Nikki followed as they tracked Daniel down the length of Main. When the street ended, he made a right and then a left and then pulled over by a small yellow house. He parked his bike near a signpost, entered through the gate, then walked through the front door without knocking.

"He must know who lives here pretty well," Hannah said.

"So?" Nikki shrugged. A few minutes later she heard a soft flutey tinkling sound trickle out from the house. "I guess Daniel plays the flute. What's the big deal about that? I don't see why he wouldn't just tell me about it."

"Come on. Playing the flute isn't exactly the most manly thing in the world," Hannah said. "Maybe he's embarrassed. Oh, and by the way, that's not a flute he's playing. It's a piccolo, which is way worse."

Nikki turned to her. "How can you tell the difference between a flute and a piccolo?" she asked. "I don't think I even know what a piccolo *is*."

"I joined the Pelican High marching band last year," Hannah said. "And a piccolo is a tiny version of a flute that plays in a higher register."

Nikki raised her eyebrows. "*You* joined the band? Why? It doesn't seem like your thing."

"Hey, you don't know this about me, but I am an *accomplished* triangle player," Hannah said proudly. "The fact that there are some very cute guys in the marching band is an added bonus. Oh, and the first trumpet player looks totally hot in his purple-and-white uniform, I might add. You should come to a football game next season. You'll see what I'm talking about."

"I think I might," Nikki said, still trying to wrap her mind around the fact that Hannah had most likely joined the band to meet boys. She could see the cheerleading squad or the track team, but the marching band? It was an odd choice. "Well, I think I've seen enough," she told her friend. "Let's get out of here."

Hannah glanced at her watch. "Are you

kidding? We just got started. Besides, I can't go back to the island now. I told your parents that I had a doctor's appointment this morning. If they see me they'll wonder what's up."

"I'm just starting to feel weird about this whole thing," Nikki said.

"How about this? We tail him until noon, then get something to eat. Maybe catch a movie, too. Deal?"

The front door to the yellow house opened and Nikki and Hannah quickly ducked behind a hedge. "See you next time, Mr. Hansen," Daniel called as he exited onto the porch. He skipped down the two steps and was on his ten-speed again in a flash.

Hannah was already on her bike. Nikki climbed on hers, too, though her heart wasn't really in it anymore. She watched Daniel make a sharp left, leading them into the town of Berkley. A few minutes later they approached the large castlelike brick building known as Berkley Preparatory. Nikki knew a few of the boys who attended the school. She even went to a winter dance there one time last year with Blair and some other girls from the Academy.

I wonder what Daniel has to do on the Berkley

campus, Nikki thought, veering onto a path leading to the main building. But as she stared at the back of Daniel's orange T-shirt she began to feel guilty again for following him.

She knew that she was just letting her insecurities get the best of her. So what if the boy ate croissants, played the piccolo, and went to Berkley three days a week? He didn't have to get her permission or check in with her 24/7. And just because Daniel hadn't kissed her yet didn't necessarily mean that he was seeing someone else.

I'm out of here, she said to herself, and pulled a quick U-turn. Unfortunately Hannah didn't realize what Nikki was doing and crashed into the side of Nikki's bike.

"Whoaaaaaa!" Hannah cried, and Nikki screamed as the two fell to the ground in a heap of tires, legs, and spokes.

Nikki groaned. She had a couple of scratches but otherwise seemed okay. "Are you all right?" she asked Hannah.

"Sure," Hannah said, rubbing an elbow. "But look who's coming."

Nikki turned to see Daniel biking toward them. "Nikki!" he called.

She sprang to her feet, embarrassed. Not only

was this the second biking incident that Daniel had been witness to, he was sure to ask what she was doing there. What would she tell him?

"I heard a crash and then I saw you guys fall," Daniel explained.

"We're fine," Nikki said, glad that Daniel had chosen not to mention the other times he'd seen her in the same predicament. "Do you know my friend Hannah?"

"Hi." Hannah, now sprawled out on the grass just off the path, gave a little wave.

"Hey." Daniel nodded at her, then glanced behind him as if he were looking for somebody. Nikki wasn't sure, but he seemed a little nervous to her. "So, um, funny running into you guys. What brings you here?" he asked.

Too bad Nikki hadn't come up with a brilliant excuse yet. "We, uh, um . . ."

Before she could even try to wing it, Daniel squinted at her, then at Hannah. "Hey, I'll bet you guys were following me! Weren't you?"

Nikki swallowed hard, knowing there was no way out of this one.

chapter 12

"We, uh, um . . ." Nikki repeated, still without a clue what to say. *How about: Yup, we were following you, and by the way, what's the deal with the croissants? I don't think so.*

"Aw, come on. Why don't you just admit it?" Daniel continued. "You *know* you were following me." He flashed a bashful grin and Nikki let out the breath she hadn't realized she was holding until then.

Is he flirting with me? she wondered. *I think so. Maybe he doesn't really know we were following him.* So she said, "Okay, okay. You got us." She tried to sound as sarcastic as possible. "We were totally following you. But it got pretty boring so we decided to spice things up with a little crash."

"Cute," Daniel said, still grinning.

"Thanks," Nikki replied, though she wasn't sure if he was talking about her or the story.

"Actually, we're here looking for this guy I know," Hannah jumped in. "His name is John. He's doing the summer acting program."

"Oh. Cool," Daniel replied.

"So what are you doing at Berkley, anyway?" Hannah continued as she got up and righted her bike. "School's out. I mean, not that you go here."

Nikki nudged Hannah. They were lucky enough not to get caught. Why did she have to go there? Hannah responded with a silent look that said, *What'd I do?*

"Oh, me? Um, I'm kind of meeting someone," Daniel said, looking around again.

Huh? Meeting someone? Not the answer Nikki wanted to hear. She was looking for something more along the lines of: *I'm visiting the stately Berkley grounds to get inspiration for a watercolor I have this sudden uncontrollable desire to paint for Nikki. Not that I know how to paint, but it would certainly be a romantic gesture.* Instead the words *I'm meeting someone . . . meeting someone . . . meeting someone . . .* flashed inside her brain over and over like one of those rolling electronic signs that she always ended up staring at in line at the bank.

Nikki felt a flash of jealousy and didn't like it.

She tried to act casual but . . . "Really? Who are you meeting?" she asked. "Maybe I know the person." She couldn't help herself.

"Nah, I doubt it," Daniel replied. He glanced at his watch. "I should probably go in a few minutes. I have a ton of stuff to do."

Now Nikki was even more curious. "Like what? Maybe Hannah and I can help. We're not doing anything now. Right, Hannah?"

"Nope. No plans here," Hannah said.

"Thanks, anyway, but I kind of have to do this stuff on my own," Daniel said. "I appreciate the offer, though." He gave Nikki one of his little punches on the arm. "Hey, Nikki, can I talk to you a sec?"

Uh-oh. "Sure!" she said, maybe a tad too brightly.

Daniel took her hand as they walked a short distance away. "You look awesome," he told her.

"Really?" Nikki glanced down at her khaki shorts and white tank. "Thanks. You, too."

"Thanks," he said. "Sorry I'm being so weird right now. I just have a lot on my mind."

"Oh?" Nikki asked. *Like your other girlfriend?* she added silently, then shoved the thought to the back of her mind. "Want to share?"

"Not yet," Daniel said, nodding. "Not until I know what's up for sure. Besides, it's kind of a surprise."

Nikki found herself smiling. Was it for her? She hoped it was. "A surprise? What is it? Am I going to like it?"

"Come on. How can I tell you and keep it a surprise? Anyway, I won't know if I can make it happen until the end of the week, so you'll have to wait until then. Okay?"

Nikki nodded, her mind whirring at the prospect. What could Daniel's surprise be? She wasn't sure she could wait until the end of the week. "So, when do you want to get together again?" she asked him, though it didn't come out sounding nearly as blasé as she wanted it to.

"That's the thing," Daniel said. "I'm going to be busy twenty-four/seven until Friday and then I have to do a family thing over the weekend."

Now Nikki wished she hadn't been the one to bring up the next date. "Oh. Yeah, well. I'm pretty busy, too. With the store and all," she said, not to seem like a total loser.

"I should be done by Sunday afternoon, though," Daniel piped up. "Can we hang out then?" He took a step closer and looked at the ground, then met her eyes bashfully. "I'd really like to see you again," he said. "I mean, if you want to see me. Do you?"

Nikki surveyed Daniel's face, then peered into the paleness of his blue eyes. They seemed so sincere. Honest. And here she was following him around, hoping to catch him in some kind of lie. For what? Because he hadn't kissed her yet? Meanwhile Daniel had been nothing but sweet and sensitive and was arranging a surprise for her. No, Nikki couldn't imagine this boy hurting her or any other girl, for that matter. It just didn't fit.

"Come by the house for dinner again," she suggested. "Then later we can take a walk to the old lighthouse on the south end of the island. If we're lucky, Mr. Cavenaugh might let us climb to the top. You can see for miles up there."

"Cool," Daniel said, nodding. Then he leaned in close and left a gentle kiss on her cheek. "I can't wait," he said.

And neither could Nikki.

Later that day Nikki was still thinking about Daniel's tender kiss as she relaxed among the colorful pillows that lined the cozy window seat in her room.

The rest of the day had gone by in a blur after she and Hannah had left Daniel. They'd gone to some burrito place in Berkley and then to a half-price matinee at the multiplex, but Nikki couldn't remember much about either even if she wanted to. She glided her fingers along the cheek where Daniel had kissed her so sweetly and felt a shiver as she imagined the feel of his soft lips on hers.

Nikki breathed in the fresh summer air as she listened to the cicadas chirp and gazed out at the quiet little street before her. In a way, Nikki was glad that she and Hannah had gone on their crazy adventure to find out the truth about Daniel because, instead of discovering some shady secret, she'd learned that the truth was what she'd always known. Daniel was a smart and caring and sometimes shy boy who liked Nikki just as much as she liked him. *Definitely not a player,* she thought, which was fine by her.

Even Hannah had commented on the chemistry between Nikki and Daniel and had said there was no denying he liked Nikki in a more-than-a-friend kind of way. And Nikki knew now that their kiss would come eventually. *You can't force these things,* she thought. *You have to be patient and let it happen naturally.* And when it did happen, she knew that it was going to be that much more amazing.

Nikki glanced at her watch. Three minutes until the IM time she'd scheduled with Blair yesterday. She couldn't wait to share the news with her friend. She rose reluctantly from her comfortable space by the window and crossed to the desk where her computer sat, and logged on. After about a minute of surfing, Blair had logged on, too.

Dare2Blair: *u there? i have official newz!!!*

YoNikkio: *I'm here. Tell me!!!!*

Dare2Blair: *the towel hut is officially multifunctional. can b used 4 ...*

> *1) hutting towels (yawn)*

> *2) hiding from muffy's 10nis racquet*

> *3) making out with my cute new bf!!!!*

YoNikkio: *LOL! You made out w/PPG?*

Dare2Blair: *Who??????*

YoNikkio: *Pool Party Guy. DUH!*

Dare2Blair: *oh. PPG = old newz. met this one at beach club. he's soooo cute. u should see him.*

YoNikkio: *2 bad we can't dbl date.*

Dare2Blair: *i guess things are going well with mr. hottie. did u kiss him yet?*

YoNikkio: *He kissed ME . . . on the cheek.*

Dare2Blair: *awwwww . . . he sounds sweet!!!!*

YoNikkio: *Totally. I wish you could meet him.*

Dare2Blair: *can't u beg S & V to come out here . . . just for weekend? bring mr. hottie! there's gonna be a big party and a bonfire on the beach on Sat. everybody's coming. will b a blast!*

YoNikkio: *Hottie can't make it. But it can't hurt if I ask the rents if I can go. Gonna call now. Hold on. BRB!*

Dare2Blair: *K.*

Nikki crossed the room to grab the phone she kept on her nightstand and dialed the number for the Italian Scallion, even though she didn't have high hopes for a yes from her parents.

"Italian Scallion. What do ya need, champ?" a girl answered.

"Hannah?" Nikki asked. "What are you doing there?"

"Oh, I felt bad for getting Vince to cover for me since it was his day off," Hannah admitted, "so I came in for a couple of hours."

"Oh. Okay. Well, is my mom around?" Nikki asked.

"Sure. Hold on a sec." Hannah must have pressed the hold button and a tinny version of "The Eye of the Tiger" sounded over the line. Nikki hummed along as she waited for her mother to pick up. The music stopped suddenly.

"What's wrong?" Mrs. Devita asked over the phone.

"Nothing, Mom," Nikki replied. "I was just online with Blair and there's this big party happening on Bella Island this Saturday and all my friends are going to be there. . . . So I was wondering if I could maybe go out for the weekend. I'll be totally responsible, I promise. Please?"

To Nikki's surprise her mom did not immediately say no. "Let me see what your father says."

Nikki heard what sounded like her mom covering the phone with a hand, then a couple of muffled voices. She tried to decipher what her parents were saying, but couldn't make it out. In a matter of minutes her mom was back on the line. *Not a good sign*, Nikki thought. She didn't even have time to come up with a rebuttal for the no her mom was about to give her.

"Your father and I discussed it and we think that since you've been working so hard at the store this summer it's okay for you to go . . ."

Yes, yes, yes! Nikki shouted silently, pumping a fist in the air.

". . . *if*," her mother continued, "your brothers go along, too."

Nikki could deal with that! "Thanks, Mom. Thanks a lot! Bye!" She hung up the phone and went back to the computer to tell Blair the good news.

Dare2Blair: *zzzzzzzzzzzzzzzzzzzzzzzzzzzz*

YoNikkio: *Wake up! Guess what? I can go . . . with my brothers, though.*

Dare2Blair: *cool! but aren't they annoying? maybe we can set one of them up w/ muffy! (ha, ha!)*

YoNikkio: *No way. No brother deserves that. Even mine.*

Dare2Blair: *OK, OK. will put you guys on the party list.*

Nikki stopped typing for a minute. There was one more person who should be on that list.

YoNikkio: *Hey, you think my friend Hannah can come too?*

chapter 13

Nikki poked through her beach bag for the millionth time on Saturday morning. *Suntan lotion, check. Towel, check. Easy reading, check. Hot new pink polka-dotted bikini, check.* Hannah and Nikki had torn through their beach attire earlier in the week and had decided that out of the ten bathing suits between them, none were right for the occasion, so they bought new ones. Nikki couldn't wait to try hers out on the Bella Island beach!

"I'm so psyched about the parrrr-taaaaay!" Vince cried from the top deck of the ferry. "Hey, Hannah, who does this remind you of?" He jumped up and raced to the front of the boat, stretching his arms out wide. "I'm the king of the world!" he cried just as the wind pulled off the camouflage fishing hat he was wearing, taking it over the side. "Oh, man!"

Nikki rolled her eyes. She was used to Vince being annoying, but this was over the top. She leaned in to Hannah, who was sitting one row ahead. "What a dork," she commented. "The *Titanic*? I mean, come *on*."

"I think it's funny," Hannah said, clearly giggling *with* Vince, not *at* him, as opposed to the rest of the passengers, who did not seem nearly as amused by his enthusiasm. "You know, it was really cool of your mom and dad to let us all go," she added, "since now they have to run the shop alone this weekend."

"Totally," Nikki agreed.

Vince bounded back to where they were sitting. "Come on, Hannah. I want to show you something." He grabbed Hannah by the hand. "Make way!" he called to nobody in particular. "Two hotties coming through! Coming through!"

To Nikki's surprise, Hannah actually went with him. She watched as Vince swooped her in his arms and pretended as if he were going to throw her overboard, while Hannah kicked and squealed.

"Oh my God," Nikki breathed, suddenly getting it. Maybe Vince was being extra obnoxious because Hannah was there. She immediately tapped Paul on the arm. He was sitting beside her wearing dark shades and bopping his head to the beat playing on his iPod.

He pulled out his right earbud. "What?"

"I figured it out. *Hannah* is the 'somebody' Vince likes, right?" Nikki asked, excited.

Paul smiled and nodded. "But you didn't hear it from me, okay?" He shoved the bud back into his ear.

This is so cool! Nikki thought, leaning back into her seat. She had asked Hannah to join them because she was so glad to be friends again, but now that she knew about Vince's crush, she was even gladder! She couldn't wait to see how the weekend played out. Whatever happened was definitely going to be interesting.

Soon the two-hour ride was coming to an end and the ferry was slowly pulling between two rows of tied pylons and into the Bella Island dock. "All ashore!" the captain called over a loudspeaker. "All passengers must go ashore! Thank you for riding the Bella Island ferry."

Nikki, Hannah, and the twins grabbed their stuff and headed out. As they disembarked the ship Nikki scanned the crowd for Blair. It wasn't hard to spot her tall, blond, and now extremely tanned friend standing on the dock chatting with one of the crew. "Blair!" she cried and waved.

147

Blair caught sight of Nikki, ran toward the group, and gave Nikki a hug. "Hey, you guys," she said. "Come on, the cook already made us a bite to eat. It's waiting at the house!"

"You didn't tell me your friend was so hot," Paul whispered to Nikki as they headed away from the jitney dock and down a narrow street lined with small pastel-colored cottages.

"Sorry, she's taken," Nikki replied. One friend dating a brother was about all she could handle. And by the way Hannah was giggling as she walked along with Vince, it looked as if Vince was going to beat out Paul on this one.

"Figures." Paul raised the volume on his iPod.

"It's just ahead," Blair said, leading them toward the water. When they reached the end of the block they came upon a supersleek modern mansion, which seemed to be made almost entirely of windows. "You guys can have your own bedrooms if you want," she said. "We have plenty to go around."

After settling in and having a quick lunch, Nikki, Blair, and the rest of the gang headed to the Bella Island beach club. Vince and Paul immediately joined a game of volleyball down on the sand while Nikki, Hannah, and Blair relaxed on lounge chairs near the pool and sipped on fruit smoothies.

"Ah, this is the life," Hannah remarked, leaning back in her chair and adjusting her aviator sunglasses.

"I know it," Blair replied. "But it's even better now that you guys are here."

Nikki nestled in her lounge and grinned, relieved to see that her two friends were getting along so well.

Blair turned to Nikki. "Hey, you didn't tell me your brother was so cute. You know, the quiet one with the iPod."

"Don't even go there," Nikki said. "One brother dating a friend is enough, and Hannah's got that covered."

"What?" Hannah asked. "I'm not going out with your brother."

"*Yet*," Blair added with a knowing nod. "You like the other one, Vince, don't you?"

"Yeah, Hannah," Nikki added. "What's the deal with you two?"

"Nothing. I mean, come on, Nikki. He's *Vince*. How could you even think I'd like *him*?" Hannah took a long sip on her strawberry-banana smoothie, then added, "He didn't say anything about me, did he?"

Nikki lowered her chair and flipped onto her stomach. "That's for me to know and you to find out," she said.

"Nikki!" Hannah swatted her lightly with her magazine. "You have to tell me!"

"Well, by the looks of things I'd say he's *very* into you, Hannah," Blair said. "See how he keeps glancing over here to see if you're watching him play volleyball?"

Nikki turned her attention to the game. Paul had just spiked the ball over the net. Then she caught Vince peeking at Hannah just as the other team returned the volley, which unfortunately whacked him in the temple. "Ow!" Luckily for the team, the ball bounced off his head and over the net again, scoring them a point.

"My man, Vince!" Paul cried and slapped his brother a high five.

"Oh, he's got it bad, Hannah," Blair said, shaking her head and laughing at Vince.

"I don't know." Hannah shrugged, but her face was pink. "I guess we'll see what happens."

Nikki turned to Blair. "So when do we get to meet your new guy?"

Blair sprayed some SPF onto her arms. "Oh, you'll see him at the party. He'll be a little late, though. Would you believe the poor guy has to work in Berkley on the weekends?"

"Aw, poor guy." Hannah pretended to pout.

"He's making a special trip out here tonight," Blair went on. "I told him so much about you, Nikki. He wanted to meet you."

"Really? That's so nice!" Nikki said, impressed.

"He's a sweetheart," Blair admitted, "and an *awesome* kisser. But you know what? I'm glad that he's not coming until later. It gives the three of us some girl time." She paused. "*So* . . . tell us about *Mr. Hottie*! How come he couldn't make it?"

"Mr. Hottie?" Hannah almost spit out her drink, giggling.

"Shut up!" Nikki said, smiling, too. "He's good," she told Blair. "He's got some family thing this weekend. I'm going to see him tomorrow. He said he's got a surprise for me."

"Any idea what it is?" Blair asked.

"No, but I'm *dying* to find out!" Nikki replied. She adjusted her shades and closed her eyes, letting herself wonder about the surprise. Then her mind drifted to Daniel himself. Then to Pelican Island and their perfect first date on that old run-down beach. *I wonder what he's doing right now*, Nikki said silently. *Is he thinking about me, too?*

"Hiyeee!" a girl's voice rang out, breaking her thoughts.

Nikki turned to see a tanned Muffy headed their way in a black-and-white sporty two-piece with a towel slung over her shoulder and that big bun on the top of her head. Then Nikki's eyes zeroed in on the girl's stomach. "Whoa, Muffy's got a total six-pack," she murmured, amazed.

"That is just *wrong*," Hannah said, looking back at Muffy, then pinching the pale skin at her waist.

"I told you she's competitive," Blair reminded Nikki. "After I hid her tennis racquet she's been running, biking, and swimming around here as if she's training for an Ironman race or something."

"There you are, Blair! I've been looking all over for you. I thought you might like to join me on a ten-mile run." She turned to Nikki. "Oh, hi-yeee, Nikki! It's so good to see you!"

"Hey . . ." Nikki suddenly realized that she only knew Blair's cousin by the name Muffy.

". . . um, this is Hannah," she said, gesturing to her friend, hoping that Muffy would introduce herself.

"Hiyeee, Hannah!" Muffy shook Hannah's hand enthusiastically. "Nice to meet you. I'm Sonia, but you can call me Sunny. Everybody does!"

Not everybody, Nikki thought, then exchanged a glance with Blair.

"So do you guys want to go for a run, or what?" Muffy asked, doing a few calf stretches. "I usually do a six-minute mile, but I promise to go slow for you guys."

"Oh, too bad! We just came back from a run," Hannah told her. "But we'll be here when you get back, okay?"

"Great!" Muffy said. "Save me a seat, will you?" She tossed her towel in Blair's direction. "Byeeeee!" Muffy set off on her jog but didn't get far. When she passed the guys playing volleyball, they coaxed her into joining the game.

"Your cousin sure has a lot of energy," Hannah said, watching the girl spike the ball hard at Paul. "But is it just me or has anybody else noticed that from behind her bun kind of looks like . . ."

"A banana-walnut muffin?" Blair asked, and all three of them cracked up.

The girls spent the rest of the day lounging in the sun and alternating swimming in the pool and going boogie-boarding in the ocean every time they got hot, while the boys played Frisbee, a quick game of soccer, and had several rides on some guy's ATV. By the time Muffy was ready to go on her run, the rest of the crew was packing it in and preparing to head back to Blair's house.

"See you at the party!" Muffy called, jogging down to the water's edge and then quickly disappearing around a sand dune.

A little rest and a raid of Blair's closet later, Nikki, Hannah, and Blair were decked out for the party.

"You look better in that pink micromini than I do, Hannah," Blair admitted as she adjusted a dangling gold earring. She was wearing supershort white shorts, a brown silk tee, and a pair of high, wedged espadrilles that laced halfway up her calves.

"Thanks," Hannah said, "but I doubt it." She smoothed on some of Nikki's strawberry lip gloss and did a little pout in the mirror of a compact.

"Practicing for Vince?" Nikki teased, and Hannah gave her a friendly shove. Then Nikki pulled her hair into a high ponytail and surveyed herself in the full-length mirror on Blair's antique wardrobe. She was looking very Audrey Hepburn in a pair of skinny black capris, a black sleeveless cowl-neck, and Blair's heels. "Ready to go?"

Vince's jaw practically hit the floor when he saw Hannah come down the stairs. *Was that a little bit of drool?* Nikki wondered as he positioned himself next to Hannah so they could chat on the walk back to the beach club for the party.

Once at the party, Nikki, Hannah, Blair, and the boys bypassed the adults by the food tables and headed straight for the crowd of kids on the dance floor. Nikki and Blair jammed together while Hannah and Paul stood laughing at Vince's goofy rendition of a break dance.

They grooved and joked for hours until the crowd began to thin out and the only people left at the party were kids under twenty years old.

"Thank *God* my parents are finally gone," Muffy said, coming up to them. She immediately removed the cardigan she had on, leaving her with a shiny silver tank that exposed her extremely firm stomach complete with cute, sparkly navel ring.

"Hey, want to dance?" Paul asked her.

"Sure!" Muffy followed him into the crowd.

"I don't know," Blair said over the music,

checking the time on her cell phone. "I'm beginning to think I've been stood up."

"Don't worry. Your guy will show," Nikki assured her, though she knew that when he did she'd be left to fend for herself. *Too bad Daniel isn't here*, she thought. *It would have been awesome for the four of us to hang out together.*

"Well, I'm going to get some punch," Blair said with a sigh. "Want some?"

"No, thanks. I'll wait for you over here." Nikki took a seat by the edge of the dance floor. A slow song had come on and she spotted Hannah and Vince, who had been dancing exclusively for most of the night, now locked in an embrace and swaying to the music.

Nikki scanned the floor for Paul, who was dancing forehead-to-forehead with Muffy and had, she noticed, miraculously convinced the girl to let down her hair. It fell into beautiful brownish-blond ringlets to the middle of her toned back. *Wow*, Nikki thought. *She should always wear it like that.*

Nikki sighed as she watched the dancers rocking back and forth to the romantic music. She'd had an awesome day on Bella Island, but the one thing that could make it perfect would be dancing with Daniel right now. *What's taking Blair so long?* she wondered. *Maybe when the hot new boyfriend gets here I'll just go home. I don't want to be a seventh wheel.*

As she waited for Blair, she had a brief fantasy about Daniel showing up. He'd pull her in his arms and whisper about how he couldn't stand to be away from her. How he'd called her parents and they'd told him where to find her.

She searched the faces in the room, hoping to find Daniel's among them, even though she knew that it was unlikely. . . . Wait a sec.

Nikki focused on the drinks table again and gasped. Blair was over there talking to a boy with a buzz cut and piercing blue eyes, who was leaning on the wall behind the table and looked a lot like Daniel. *No, it can't be him . . . can it?* she wondered, squinting her eyes. *Yes, it is! He's probably asking Blair where to find me!*

Nikki practically leaped out of her seat and waved the two down as she crossed the room. But they didn't see her. No, they couldn't have, because now they were turning for the door and heading outside. . . .

When Nikki got closer she noticed something else. Blair and Daniel were leaving the party together.

And they were holding hands.

chapter 14

No, Nikki said to herself. *You have to be seeing things. You have to! Maybe it's not really Daniel. It couldn't be Daniel, right? He said he was doing a family thing this weekend.*

Hoping it was all some big awful mistake, Nikki felt sick to her stomach as she left the party, too — because it *was* Daniel. As she watched him and Blair exit the beach house onto the patio by the pool, a barrage of questions surged through her mind. Are Blair and Daniel together? Is Daniel the cute new boyfriend that Blair was talking about? How could this be?

Keeping a safe distance behind, Nikki skulked in the shadows as Daniel led Blair onto the beach. She watched as they stopped to say hello to a few of the kids sitting by a huge bonfire, then strolled down the beach for some privacy.

Now Nikki was approaching the bonfire, still staring after her best friend and the guy she thought was her boyfriend. A sandy-haired boy Nikki recognized from Berkley Prep, Stuart something, asked her a question but she didn't catch what he'd said. "Huh?" she asked. "What?"

"I asked if you wanted to hang out and toast a few marshmallows with us," Stuart said, pointing to the group of couples around the fire. A guy with short blond dreads was strumming on a guitar and singing an unplugged version of "Smells Like Teen Spirit" while his girlfriend gazed at him as if he were a god. Apparently Stuart was the only single one in the group. "Come on, it'll be fun." He held out a twig for her to take.

"Oh. No, thanks," Nikki replied, grateful that he'd decided not to press the issue and had left her there. She wanted to get closer to Blair and Daniel — to hear their conversation — but as she inspected their body language, she knew that it didn't matter what they were saying. Daniel was now facing Blair, holding both of her hands in his, as they whispered and laughed underneath the silvery moonlight. Nikki knew that at any moment he'd pull Blair close and kiss her softly on the lips — the kiss that Nikki had been dreaming of for weeks.

Nikki turned away just as the tears began to

burn her eyes and slide down her cheeks. She didn't want to see the kiss. She couldn't. *A family thing*, she thought bitterly, feeling foolish for believing every word that Daniel had told her. *Hannah was right about him having a girlfriend. I just didn't want to see it. . . .*

"So, what are you going to do, Nikki?" Hannah whispered early the next morning.

Last night, after seeing Daniel and Blair together, Nikki had run back into the party and informed Vince, Paul, and Hannah that she was tired. Then she'd headed back to Blair's house early to have a good cry and to go to bed. She'd woken up several times during the night. Around six A.M. she knew she was awake for good, so she padded into Hannah's bedroom to talk and told her the whole story.

"I guess I really just want to go home," Nikki admitted. "But the first boat isn't out of here for a few hours."

"Do you think Blair knows that her guy is *your* guy?" Hannah asked. "I mean, maybe before I met her I'd assume it, but now . . . she couldn't, could she? Not if she believed what Daniel told her about having a job on the weekends."

Nikki shook her head slowly. "I don't know," she said. "I don't *think* Blair would be that shady, but then again, I can't really trust my judgment lately."

"Me neither," Hannah admitted. "I can't believe I like your brother . . . but I do. He was so sweet at the dance last night." She paused. "But listen, if this is too weird for you — me and your brother, I mean — I don't have to date him."

"Are you kidding me? I'm psyched for you guys," Nikki said. "Besides, if Vince is seeing you he won't have time to bug me," she added with a shrug. "It's like an added bonus."

"Are you sure?" Hannah asked, eyeing Nikki carefully. "Because we're finally friends again and I don't want anything to come between us — ever. We should talk about stuff, okay?"

Nikki nodded. "I feel exactly the same way. It's good to talk." She leaned in and gave Hannah a huge hug, so glad to have her best friend back for good.

When they broke apart, Hannah stared at Nikki, concerned. "You know, you should probably have it out with Blair at some point before we leave," she advised her. "To get her side of things."

"I know I should," Nikki said. "I just don't know how to start the conversation." With that, she rolled out of Hannah's bed and headed for the door.

"Where are you going?" Hannah asked.

"To take a walk on the beach. I need to clear my head. Get some perspective before everything comes out in the open."

"Good idea. I'll come with you." Hannah got up, too, and searched through her duffel for a pair of shorts.

"No, that's okay." Nikki held up a hand to stop her. "I think I need to be alone for a while."

"You sure?" Hannah asked, sounding doubtful.

Nikki nodded. "I'll be okay." She was about to leave, then turned back to Hannah. "Do me a favor — don't say anything about this to Vince or Paul yet. If I know my brothers, they're liable to track Daniel down and beat him to a pulp before I even get back."

"I won't," Hannah promised.

"Thanks," Nikki said, so grateful that Hannah was there for her. She tiptoed back to the room next door and slipped into a pair of shorts, a T-shirt, and her flip-flops, then headed out the sliding doors off the kitchen and onto the deck overlooking the ocean. A few steps later she was on the sand.

The morning air was cool and a bit damp, leaving a trail of fog just off the shore. Nikki breathed the fresh air deeply and, when she reached the ocean's edge, slipped off her shoes to let the cool water flow easily between her toes.

Nikki walked not knowing exactly where she'd end up, just that she couldn't stop until she got there. She swished the water with every stride, considering the situation. It was too hard to think about Daniel specifically. Nikki had liked him so much and he had been a total creep all along — fooling not only her but her family as well. Instead she thought about Blair, and how hurt she'd be if it turned out that she *didn't* know the truth about Daniel. Then she thought about friendship and how devastated *Nikki* would feel if it turned out that Blair knew that her cute new boyfriend was Nikki's "Mr. Hottie." How would Nikki ever trust another human being after having been the butt of a sick joke like that?

Nikki shook off the thought and pressed on down the beach, trying to drink in the beauty of the scenery rather than stew in the awful betrayal she was feeling. She noticed a figure in the distance that seemed to be moving in her direction. *I guess there's someone else crazy enough to be out this early reflecting on the atrocities of human nature.* She decided it was time to turn back — time to get this over with. Have the talk with Blair, then get herself off of Bella Island and back home where she belonged.

As Nikki marched along the water and back to Blair's house she thought she heard someone calling her name. She looked back and saw the figure running. No, not a figure. A boy. Daniel. He was waving his arms in the air, trying to capture her attention.

No way did Nikki want to talk to him now. She spun around again and hurried faster to the house. She was almost there.

"Nikki!" Daniel called. "Wait up!"

She didn't turn, hoping he'd go away. But he didn't.

"Nikki," he said, reaching for her arm and breathing hard from running. "I . . . why . . . didn't . . . you stop?"

Give me a break, Nikki thought, but she decided to go along with it. See what kind of lie he'd come up with. She stopped and looked at him. "Wow,

Daniel, I didn't realize it was you. What are you doing here?" she asked, blinking innocently. "I thought you had a family thing."

"I did," he replied. "The thing was on Bella Island."

Oh, he's quick, Nikki thought, *but not quick enough*. "With your aunt Winnie?" she asked. "I thought she rarely left her house."

Daniel squinted at her and tilted his head. "Nikki, is something wrong?"

Nikki rolled her eyes. Was he *joking*? Did he really think she was that stupid? "Enough with the games, Daniel. I *saw* you last night . . . on the beach. With Blair."

"Oh." Daniel ran a hand over his head. "I see how that might look bad."

"No kidding." Nikki turned and marched up the beach, away from the water and to the glass mansion.

"Nikki, please," Daniel said, following her. "Let me explain. It's not how it seems."

Nikki stopped. "Come on, you can think of something better than that, can't you?" She stared coolly into his eyes.

"Nikki." Daniel held both of her arms and

she glanced away — down at the sand, at the deck on Blair's house, anywhere but into Daniel's eyes. "I'm telling you the truth," he said. "My family and Blair's family have known each other for years. Our parents thought it would be cute to see us together. Neither of us wanted to do it but . . ."

"I really don't want to hear this," Nikki said, trying to pull away.

Daniel held on to her and continued. "Our parents wouldn't take no for an answer. So I came out here. Went to Blair. I told her that I already have a girlfriend. . . . *You*."

"I *am*? I mean . . ." Nikki looked at him. "You *did*?"

Daniel nodded. "Blair said that was fine by her because she had a new boyfriend," he added.

"So, you're not Blair's new boyfriend?" she asked slowly.

"No way," Daniel said. "Blair's nice, but I don't like her like that. And she doesn't like me, either. And then last night I found out that you and Blair are friends. That's what we were talking about when you saw us on the beach, Nikki. We were talking about you. And how beautiful and funny and awesome you are. And how she thought it would be so cool if I came over to see you this morning."

Nikki turned and gazed at him. She *wanted* it to be true and it *sounded* true, but . . . "What about all those days when I couldn't reach you? You didn't return my calls. What was I supposed to think?"

"Oh." Daniel took a few steps away. "I was hoping you wouldn't ask me about that."

Nikki folded her arms across her chest. "Well, I did."

"Yeah, um, this is kind of embarrassing." Daniel took a deep breath and glanced at her. "I've been taking a few extra classes and . . . all right, I'll just say it. I've been practicing for the school band, okay?" he admitted. "The conductor offered to tutor me, I mean *torture* me, this summer."

"Wait. You're in *band*?" Nikki asked, trying not to giggle. Now she could sort of relate to Hannah's fascination with musicians in ugly uniforms.

Daniel nodded sheepishly. "Not by choice, believe me," he said. "It's a requirement for this school I'm trying to get into. I wanted to play the drums but the only instrument left was . . . man, I *hate* the piccolo! It's so humiliating!"

Nikki couldn't hold back any longer. She laughed and so did Daniel.

"The piccolo, huh? That's great," she said, happy that it was making sense now. "You know, you didn't have to be embarrassed to tell me," Nikki added, figuring she should probably come clean herself. "I already knew about it."

"You did?" Daniel asked, surprised. "How?"

"Hey, Nikki! Daniel!" Blair was on the deck of the mansion and was waving them over. "Come on in. The cook is making crepes for breakfast — any kind you want!" A tall, tan, and very cute surfer-looking guy with longish sandy hair emerged from the house and slipped an arm around Blair's waist. "And I want you guys to meet Jared!" she added. "He just got in on the boat!"

"Let's go get something to eat and I'll tell you all about it," Nikki suggested, taking his hand and walking toward the house, happy that this whole mess was all a stupid misunderstanding. Daniel was the guy Nikki had thought he was all along.

Daniel stopped walking and pulled on her

hand. "I have something else to tell you. I was going to save it for later, but I can't wait anymore. It's the surprise I was telling you about."

The surprise? Nikki had forgotten all about it! "What is it?"

"Remember that day you saw me on the Berkley campus?" Daniel asked, and she nodded. "I was totally stressing because I was about to take a test — an entrance exam for the new school I want to go to. My parents said that if I passed it and took the extra classes I needed to get in this summer — including Band — I wouldn't have to go to military school anymore."

Nikki gasped. "And did you?" she asked.

"Yup." Daniel grinned. "No more uniforms, no more extreme haircuts . . . I'm starting Berkley Prep in September!"

"Whoa!" Nikki yelped when Daniel picked her up and twirled her around and around. "That's so awesome!" she said, knowing that this meant they'd get to see each other even after the summer was over.

"Guys, are you coming or what?" Hannah called from the deck with Vince in tow.

"Be right there!" Nikki cried, and Hannah and

Vince went back inside. "Are you ready?" she asked Daniel.

"One more thing," he whispered, gently brushing a few strands of hair away from her face. He held her tenderly in his arms, and when he leaned in, Nikki knew what was about to happen.

She closed her eyes and tilted her head, ready to kiss her boyfriend for the very first time. Their first real kiss. The first of many more to come.

Do you  bikinis, too?

Try these two on for size!

From HE'S WITH ME
by Tamara Summers

"Can't you just say no?" Colin asked Jake.

"Even I know the answer to that," Lexie said. "Nobody says no to Bree." Lexie understood exactly what Jake was worried about. She'd been avoiding Bree since elementary school. If you stayed far under her radar, you could slip by unnoticed and unharmed, but if you popped into her line of sight in any way, she would rip you to shreds with one flick of her French-tipped nails.

"Doomed," Jake muttered. "Dooooomed."

"All right," Colin said. "Tell her you already have a girlfriend."

Jake thought for a minute. "Like, long distance? I don't think she'll buy that. Plus it's only been a week since school ended. Where would I have picked up a girlfriend in a week?"

"I dunno." Colin shrugged. "You could tell her you're dating Lexie."

Lexie was so, so, SO glad that Colin had his eyes glued to the camera controls and didn't see her expression. Jake kept his arms over his face, so he didn't notice, either. She felt like she might faint. There was a really awkward pause, and Lexie wondered if she was supposed to make a joke here.

She started to say, "As if —" at the same time as Jake said, "Well, I —" and they both stopped.

"What were you going to say?" he said. He put his arms down and tilted his head back to look at her.

"Um, just . . . as if she'll believe that."

"Why?" Colin said. Lexie wished Jake would say something, but he just kept looking at her.

"Well, if you think Bree is out of his league, then I'm in another solar system, aren't I?" she tried to joke.

"Actually, it might work," Jake said. Lexie bit her tongue, she was so surprised.

"Sure it will," Colin said. "Lexie will be at

Summerlodge, too, so Bree can see you're together. And it's only for a little while, until Bree gets over you. And it's not like there's anyone Lexie wants to date, so you're hardly putting a dent in her love life. Right, Lexie?"

That's nice. Thanks, Colin.

"What do you say, Lexie?" Jake said, rolling over onto his stomach and propping his elbows on the floor and his chin in his hands adorably. "Want to be my pretend girlfriend?" His eyes were like storm clouds, big and unstoppable and irresistible.

Lexie, this is what you've been dreaming about.

Correction: This is a strange parody of what you've been dreaming about. Is this really what you want? Being Jake's pretend girlfriend?

Yeah, sure, okay. Close enough!

"Okay," she said, feeling dizzy. "I mean, it'll be tough pretending to like you, but I guess I can take one for the team. Right?"

"You're my knight in shining armor," Jake said, getting up and kneeling on the couch next to her. *Right* next to her. "My hero, my warrior princess," he said, taking her hand. "My King Kong." He pressed her hand to his heart. She could actually feel it beating through the soft fabric of his shirt. It was going really fast. Nearly as fast as hers, but he was an athlete, so it probably went that fast all the time.

"Okay, here are the Rules of Pretend Dating Lexie," she said. "You need to STOP comparing me to a giant gorilla."

"What are the other rules?" he asked. He was still holding her hand against his chest.

"That's the only one," she said. Was her voice shaking? Could he tell? "So far. I'll keep you posted as others come up."

He grinned. "I'll look forward to it."

"Okay," Colin said, standing up. "I think I've figured out how to change it to night recording. Let's go test it in the shed." He picked up a flashlight and headed for the stairs. Lexie couldn't believe her own twin hadn't noticed how much she was blushing. She wanted to stay where she was forever, but she pulled her hand free and scrambled off the couch.

"Great, okay," she said. "Sounds like fun." She looked back from the doorway. "Coming, Jake?"

"You bet," he said, standing up and stretching. "Where my girlfriend goes, I go."

Lexie shivered.

I always thought my first boyfriend would be Jake. But I never thought it would only be pretend. . . .

From WHAT'S HOT
by Caitlyn Davis

"I love guys who wear flip-flops."

Holly Bannon watched a guy amble across the large lawn at Mrs. Whittingham's estate, where she and her best friend, Ainslee, were attending a "Welcome to the Club" party. They were both working at the Ridgemont Country Club for the summer, starting the next day.

"I don't know. Isn't he a little short for you?" Holly asked Ainslee, who was nearly five foot nine.

"Crudités?" A caterer holding a tray paused in front of them.

"Sorry?" Holly asked.

"It's an appetizer," Ainslee said. "Take one. Très delicious." She grabbed one from the tray and popped it into her mouth.

"Thanks," Holly told the caterer. She carefully took a small bite of the celery, nibbling the edge. She watched as another guy jogged across the lawn, toward the shuffleboard court on the other side of the in-ground pool.

Shuffleboard, thought Holly. *Who ever even heard of it before tonight?*

"How about him, Ains?" she asked.

"Mmm . . . no." Ainslee shook her head. "Don't like the hat."

"Really?" Holly took another look at him. "You're too picky. I think he's cute. Or he was, but I can't really see him anymore."

"He's all right, but I hate the way he runs. Anyway. We're going to meet so many guys this summer. We don't have to settle for someone who's just sort of okay and wears a baseball cap sideways," Ainslee declared. "My mom always says, 'Never settle.' "

Holly wasn't quite convinced. "Are you sure we're going to meet *that* many guys?" It wasn't as if the Ridgemont Country Club was strictly for high-school guys. *Although that would be cool*, she thought. Except then she couldn't belong to it, which wouldn't be cool at all.

"Are you joking? We are, definitely. I mean, for sure we'll meet more than we did last summer — what were we doing again?" Ainslee tapped the side of her head. "Oh yeah. Now I remember. *Nothing.* For *weeks.*"

"But we're going to be too busy working this year to hang out just looking for guys," Holly said.

"Working? Come on. I'll be playing tennis occasionally. You'll be pouring pops. That's only thirty or forty hours a week. That leaves us plenty of time to socialize. And by socialize, I mean flirt."

"There's just one problem. Do we know how to flirt?" Holly asked.

Ainslee laughed. "Not well. But we'll learn."

Holly had to admit that they'd both scored in getting jobs at Ridgemont for the summer. It was the best place to work, because students from all around the area were hired as staff. It was a chance to hang out with a big crowd and meet someone new, and there were lots of parties over the summer, too. Also, the club's owner, Mrs. Whittingham, believed in letting employees have access to the gym, the golf course, the tennis courts — and, most important to Holly, the pool.

Holly pushed Ainslee's arm. "Okay, so. Moving on. Have you thought of a decent way for us to meet those guys yet?"

Ainslee looked around the party. "We're new here, right? So maybe we don't know where everything is. You could go ask them for directions to the bathroom."

"Are you serious?" Holly wasn't about to embarrass herself like that. "Right. Why don't *you*?" she asked.

"No, you."

Holly shook her head. "No."

"Okay, then. Grab a tray. Go over and offer them something to eat," Ainslee suggested. "Then introduce yourself. It'll be natural because you can say you're working for the kitchen this summer, and this is part of the job. Go on. Do it."

"Won't that be kind of obvious?" asked Holly.

"Everything's going to feel obvious to *us*, but it won't be to them. They're guys," Ainslee said. "They don't notice anything. And remember— we said we were going to be more bold this summer. So. Go."

"Right. Okay. We did say that." Trying to look

casual, Holly ambled over to the tent where the caterers had set up.

"Excuse me," she said to a man wearing the standard black-and-white catering outfit. "Would it be okay if I walked around with a tray of something?"

"A tray of something?" He frowned at her. "Why would you want to do that?"

"Well, see, I'm working in the kitchen this summer — the, uh, club café — and I need the practice," Holly said with a smile.

He stared at her as if she had lost her mind. "But . . . the club's café doesn't have waited tables."

Did he have to be such a know-it-all? Holly wondered. "I know, I know, but still. It's customer service, right, so it's good practice. Would it be okay?"

"I suppose. I'll have a seat for ten seconds while you do that. Here, I was just about to bring these out. Shrimp puffs. Make the rounds," he said. "But don't let that group over there take them all." He pointed to the group of guys that Holly planned on making a beeline toward.

"No problem. I'll watch them like a hawk." Holly lifted the tray. "Thanks! This will be great."

"Okay, whatever." The caterer sank onto a folding chair, looking spent.

This is like something out of a movie, Holly thought as she approached the group of guys beside the pool. *But it works in the movies, so why not here?*

She assumed as casual an expression as possible while she walked up to them. She took a deep breath to compose herself. *Don't say anything stupid,* she told herself. *Just make eye contact and smile.*

She walked up to the edge of the group and stopped. The guys were joking and laughing about something and didn't notice her at first. *Maybe I should just step away,* she thought as she stared at the back of Extremely Cute Guy's blue T-shirt, which was sort of extremely cute even from the back. *Forget this whole idea.*

Holly cleared her throat. "Excuse me, would you care for a —"

Extremely Cute Guy quickly turned around. The shuffleboard stick he had perched on his shoulder came flying straight at Holly's face.

"Ack!" Holly jumped out of the way — and into the pool, feetfirst.

Somehow, because she landed in the shallow

end, she managed to hold the tray upright. "Shrimp puff?" she offered as Extremely Cute Guy stared down at her, his friends gathering behind him.

He didn't jump in to rescue her.

He didn't hold out his hand and pull her toward the edge. He didn't apologize for nearly making her lose an eye.

Instead, he just said, "Swim much?" and laughed with his friends. Loudly. At her.

Holly felt like tossing the tray — along with the contents of the pool — back in his face. *Swim much?* What kind of a thing was that to say to a person who nearly drowned — of embarrassment, anyway?

Well, it was one way to meet guys. Maybe not the *best* way, and maybe not the ones you planned on meeting, but still.

To Do List: Read all the Point books!

By Aimee Friedman

☐ South Beach
0-439-70678-5

☐ French Kiss
0-439-79281-9

☐ Hollywood Hills
0-439-79282-7

By Hailey Abbott

☐ Summer Boys
0-439-54020-8

☐ Next Summer: A
Summer Boys Novel
0-439-75540-9

☐ After Summer: A
Summer Boys Novel
0-439-86367-8

☐ Last Summer: A
Summer Boys Novel
0-439-86725-8

By Claudia Gabel

☐ In or Out
0-439-91853-7

By Nina Malkin

☐ 6X: The
Uncensored
Confessions
0-439-72421-X

☐ 6X: Loud, Fast,
& Out of Control
0-439-72422-8

☐ Orange Is the
New Pink
0-439-89965-6

Point

POINTCKLT